THE JUDAS FACTOR

TED ALLBEURY

THE MYSTERIOUS PRESS

New York • London

MYSTERIOUS PRESS EDITION

This Mysterious Press Edition is published by arrangement with the author, and was originally published in Great Britain by New English Library.

Cover design by Rolf Erickson
Cover illustration by Sonja Lamut and Nenad Jakesevic

Mysterious Press books are published in association with
Warner Books, Inc.
666 Fifth Avenue
New York, N.Y. 10103
A Warner Communications Company

Printed in the United States of America

Originally published in hardcover by The Mysterious Press.
First Mysterious Press Paperback Printing: March, 1989

10 9 8 7 6 5 4 3 2 1

Critical Acclaim For Ted Allbeury
and
THE JUDAS FACTOR

"In the unlikely event John le Carré and Ross Thomas were to collaborate, the product might well resemble Ted Allbeury's *The Judas Factor.*"

—*Los Angeles Times*

☆

"Mr. Allbeury is a writer of espionage novels that often soar above the genre."

The New Yorker

☆

"Allbeury's novels have won a reputation not only for versimilitude but for crisp, economical narration and high drama . . . there's no better craftsman."

—*Chicago Sun-Times*

☆

"No one picks through the intelligence maze with more authority or humanity than Allbeury."

—*Sunday Times*, London

☆

"Ted Allbeury is perhaps the best, most authentic and skilled spy novelist in a very crowded business."

—*Toronto Sun*

☆

"The British spy story has an articulate exponent in Ted Allbeury . . . a fine entertainer as well as a most knowledgable chronicler of espionage."

—*New York Times Book Review*

☆

"Ted Allbeury is a classic writer of espionage fiction."

—Len Deighton

☆

"A master of the genre . . . he writes as sensitively on matters of the heart as he does on cloak-and-dagger derring-do."

—*Los Angeles Times*

Also by Ted Allbeury

A CHOICE OF ENEMIES
SNOWBALL
PALOMINO BLONDE
THE SPECIAL COLLECTION
THE ONLY GOOD GERMAN
MOSCOW QUADRILLE
THE MAN WITH THE PRESIDENT'S MIND
THE LANTERN NETWORK**
CONSEQUENCE OF FEAR
THE ALPHA LIST
THE TWENTIETH DAY OF JANUARY
THE LONELY MARGINS
CODEWORD CROMWELL
THE SECRET WHISPERS
THE OTHER SIDE OF SILENCE
SHADOW OF SHADOWS
ALL OUR TOMORROWS
PAY ANY PRICE
THE GIRL FROM ADDIS
NO PLACE TO HIDE
CHILDREN OF TENDER YEARS
THE SEEDS OF TREASON*
THE STALKING ANGEL*

***Published by**
THE MYSTERIOUS PRESS

**forthcoming

This book is for Dr Martin Robards – consultant paediatrician at Pembury Hospital, Kent – whose skill and care over many years has made it possible for my daughter Lisa who had Still's Disease, to be transformed from a five year old with permanently painful swollen joints to a happy, active and very beautiful fifteen year old. It comes with love from us all.

TED ALLBEURY

Chapter 1

THE PIANIST was playing 'Ain't Misbehavin'' and if he'd been listening Fats Waller wouldn't have been offended. But if he *had* been listening he'd have been the only one in the club who was.

The girl looked across the table as the man refilled her wine glass.

'*Are* you a Jew, Charles?'

The man didn't look up as he filled his own glass slowly and carefully.

'No. What made you ask?'

'Daddy says you are in his letter.'

'Good old Daddy. Cheers.'

He held up his glass to her before he drank.

'You can't just dismiss it like that. He's been checking on you. I told you he would.'

'Did he check on your husband before he married you?'

'That's different. Our families knew one another. We moved in the same social circles.'

'The ones where husbands beat up their wives?'

He saw the flush on her cheeks. It had been unsporting but she'd asked for it. And he was irritated by the question. Her grey eyes were antagonistic as she looked at his face.

'You're not much help. I'm only trying to get things straightened out.'

He reached over the table and put his hand gently on hers. 'I'm sorry, Judy. I'm not being difficult but it's pointless you trying to convince him. He wants you to go back to your husband. Your father-in-law is an influential man and it doesn't do your father's career a lot of good when his daughter lights out to do her own thing. And if she ends up with another man he ain't going to call for champagne and hope that she'll be happier the second time around.'

'You'd like him if you met him. He's only trying to protect me.'

'How old are you, sweetie?'

'You know how old I am. I'm twenty-nine.'

'Maybe it's time you decided things for yourself.'

'I *have* decided, Charles. You know that. As soon as I can get a divorce I want to marry you. You're what I want.'

He looked across at her face and said softly, 'Why do you want me?'

She shrugged her shoulders, and half-smiled. 'You're my rock, Charles. My protector. I'd be lost without you.'

'D'you want to dance?'

She looked round the smoke filled room of the club and then back at his face. She shook her head slowly. 'Why do you hang on to this place?'

He smiled. 'Greed. It makes me money.'

For a moment she looked back at him, and then hesitantly she opened her handbag and passed him an envelope. He saw the US stamp and the New York postmark. It was addressed to her. He guessed it was from her father. He looked up at her.

'D'you want me to read it?'

She nodded, and he took the single page out and folded it open. The New York address of her parents was embossed on the expensive paper. He was the UN representative of what had once been a small part of the British Empire. The handwriting was neat and clenched up, with Greek 'es' and a lot of underlining.

Ma chère Judy,

Needless to say, I have been much disturbed by the news in your letters. You seem to have swallowed everything this man says, 'holus-bolus'. I have had some of his 'facts' checked out. I understand from *English* friends of mine that he has grossly exaggerated his position at the Foreign Office. For many years he was employed on minor consular activities, mainly the issuing of passports and trade documents. The lowest of the low.

As for his self-styled linguistic abilities, nobody who left school aged fifteen is capable of learning foreign languages. He *claims* to speak Polish and Russian, no doubt aware that these are languages you are not able to test him on. You remember Kretski, the Ambassador at the Polish Embassy when I was in London? Get him to invite you both to one of their minor receptions. He would check his languages for you.

Whilst I find it is correct that he has not been married I find this in itself suspicious. A man of his age must have very 'good' reasons for being single. As for what you referred to as his being owner of a popular night club my heart *sinks*. If it were the best in London, is this the background you wish to be part of? And when I am told on good authority that it is in fact a tenth-rate club in Soho, patronised by the criminal element and prostitutes, I wonder how you could be so easily deceived by this man. You make him out to be some sort of Sir Galahad. I see him more as a typical central European, Jew-boy entrepreneur. Is this where your expensive education has led you? Your previous diversions during your marriage were at least with people from your own circle, but this '*nostalgie de la boue*' is, quite frankly, inexplicable.

Why don't you come over to New York for a few months and consider, without pressure, your position? Your mother and I are 'ad idem' on all this.'

Your loving father

Anders slowly folded the letter, slid it back into its envelope and reached over to put it beside her plate. He lit a cigarette before he spoke.

'There's food for thought there, my love.'

'He's only trying to help me.'

'Or somebody. When are you going to fix for us to go to Weymouth Street?'

'Weymouth Street? Why Weymouth Street?'

'That's where the Polish Embassy is.'

Her eyes brightened. 'You mean you'll go there with me?'

'I don't mind jumping through a couple of hoops if it'll make you happy.'

'I love you, Charles.'

'And I love you.'

'I'd better be going. I promised to call in at the French Embassy after dinner. The Couve de Mourvilles are over for the week and I was at school with their daughter when Daddy was in Paris.'

'I'll walk out with you for a taxi.'

She blushed. 'I'm going by tube.'

In his lap, out of sight, he took out five ten-pound notes from his wallet and folding them over he passed them to her.

'I can't keep taking money off you, Charles. I really can't.'

He stood up and moved her chair back as she stood too, and they walked up the dimly lit stairs to the grubby foyer and out into the street. He walked with her through to Charing Cross Road and waved down a taxi that had just dropped a fare at Leicester Square underground station. He kissed her as he held open the door and stood waiting until the taxi drove off.

He looked at his watch. It was almost ten o'clock and he crossed the street and walked through to Leicester Square. The square was crowded. The usual group of dropouts, a police car with its blue lamp flashing, its occupants sitting and watching. Their faces had that strange immobility that policemen's faces have when they are waiting for something to happen, contemplating the people walking by, wondering whether it would be a drunken fight or an unconscious heroin addict that they had to deal with first. It was too early for knifings and gang fights, and break-ins would come over the radio.

Anders was walking against the stream, but he was in no hurry. He wasn't going anywhere. He just felt a need to be out in the world. Not having to talk, not having to think. Walking amongst strangers who weren't part of his life, and for whom he had not the slightest responsibility. At Piccadilly Circus he just stood. Watching the traffic and the people. The touts, the pimps and the pushers, and the well-dressed middle-class who had just come out of the cinema, still humming the tunes from the re-run of *Gigi*.

Tadeusz Charles Anders was a big-built man, but his six feet one inch made his broad shoulders look less broad and his big face look less aggressive. He wasn't handsome, but he was certainly attractive. It was an old-fashioned manly face that could have earned him good money in Hollywood. A John Wayne face. Lived in, with hard eyes but a benevolent mouth, and hair that was black and wiry. Those who looked carefully at faces would have said that it wasn't an English face. And they would have been right. His father had been Polish and his mother a Scot, and the two sets of flamboyant genes showed not only in his face but in his temperament. There was no doubt that the Polish genes were dominant, and they and a few other factors in his early life had been responsible for his troubles in SIS. They valued and used his physical strength, even his wild outbreaks of anger when provoked. But as an established officer of SIS they saw him as a potential source of embarrassment. He was the stuff that Parliamentary Questions are made of. He still worked for them, and it was SIS cash that had funded the setting up of his club. As an undercover man he was invaluable. Available for operations that were never minuted, which could be denied as having anything to do with MI6 and the Foreign Office. And the sleazy club acted as a letter-drop, a safe-house and a meeting place.

Tad Anders had been born in the small Northumbrian town of Morpeth, the son of a refugee from Poland who had joined the Free Polish Army. Captain Anders had been killed in the assault on Monte Cassino and from that time the boy's mother had tried to be both father and mother. Born in poverty in Glasgow she had the gift of counting her blessings. There was a considerable Polish colony in Morpeth and young Anders learned Polish at the little Polish school, and spent his free time with other children of his age. He was good at games and bright at his school-work, and was welcome in many homes.

His mother was a teacher at the local primary school. She was a patient, competent teacher, but it was obvious to all that her son was the centre of her life. It was equally obvious that his mother's love and devotion were appreciated by the boy. He did the man's jobs around the house and was consulted about the household budget. She didn't spoil him, although it was an easy-going relationship on both sides. They were able to take each other's affection for granted.

In the summer after his eighteenth birthday they had the letter offering him a place at Newcastle University. Neither of them realised what a climactic effect that brief, formal note would have on both their lives.

Maggie Anders' virtues were not altogether rare for northern England and the Border counties, but they were rare enough to be prized, particularly when they went hand in hand with a lively personality and an attractive woman. There had been several interested men but she had never let their interest prosper beyond an arm's-length friendliness. She accepted invitations to agricultural shows and sometimes a play or concert in Newcastle but the men were never invited to her home. She liked them all or she wouldn't have accepted their invitations, but there was one, a man who farmed near Alnwick, who was her particular favourite. He was a calm, patient, smiling man whose wife had been killed in a road accident towards the end of the war. They had met at the house of a mutual friend and had taken to each other instantly. It had been almost a year before they met again and there had been only a score or so of meetings since. But when she told him the good news in the letter from the University he had asked her to marry him. And with her son well on the way to independence she had accepted.

Maggie had waited two days before she told the boy, after they had finished their evening meal together. She made it clear that it would never make any difference to them – they'd always be the same.

The wedding was a few weeks later and Tadeusz was to

stay with his aunt while the couple had a few days honeymoon in Edinburgh. There were many people at the wedding from both Alnwick and Morpeth, for the couple were much liked and respected. The boy stood with his aunt and nieces as the couple were photographed on the church steps. Like the others, he saw the tears on Maggie's cheeks, but unlike the others he couldn't bear that she was smiling too. And her new husband had his arm round her.

Everything he had went into the old armykit-bag, including his father's medals from the small glass-fronted showcase. He went down to London the same day and two days later he was starting his recruit training at Caterham barracks, saying 'Yes, trained soldier' and 'No, trained soldier' to his three-month seniors in the Coldstream Guards. He had remembered a sign on the Great North Road, just a few miles from Morpeth: Coldstream 22 miles. He didn't reveal his true name and age until he was commissioned.

In some ways the army is a quite kindly orphanage, and it liked the courage and ability of the young lieutenant who absorbed so readily all they had to teach him. Because of his Polish he was transferred to the Intelligence Corps who sent him on a Russian course and by the usual process of snakes and ladders he became one of the more experienced and valued officers in SIS, the Secret Intelligence Service, MI6. Singleness of purpose was the phrase most often used by his various superiors. He never saw nor heard of his mother again. He never talked about his childhood and almost succeeded in never thinking about it. He felt he'd learned a lesson about women from his mother, and he was glad he'd learned it early. No woman would ever again get the chance to bring back that sudden cold that gripped his limbs, the feeling of darkness and a rushing wind. The feeling that the lights had all gone out. Loneliness.

He was well liked by men and women. Despite his looks, his vitality and his obvious intelligence, for some reason men never saw him as a rival. For the same reasons, many young women saw him as a husband, and even more saw him as a lover.

Anders bought a Final edition of the *Evening Standard* and looked at the front page. They were going to re-open the Suez Canal in June. Turning to the Stop Press he checked the result of the last race at Sandown. Crown Prince had won by a length at 11–1 so Chalky White had been right. He said he'd had it from the horse's 'connections' and they obviously knew what they were talking about. It was beginning to drizzle and he turned and walked back towards the club.

He walked up Charing Cross Road and turned into one of the alleys just before Great Newport Street. The red neon sign outside the club door announced that it was the entrance to the Kama Sutra Club, and a flashing arrow pointed the way.

Inside the door was a small reception area complete with a well-worn flowered Wilton carpet that went well with the blistered brown paint on the walls. On the far wall were two rows of crude hooks for jackets and coats, and on the left was a reception counter with a black GPO phone and a red internal phone. On the wall behind the counter was a faded, handwritten notice that said Members Only. And taking pride of place were two centrefolds from girlie magazines Sellotaped to an otherwise empty notice board.

Anders stopped to talk to the young man behind the counter.

'How are we doing tonight, Tony?'

'Pretty good, Mr Anders. We're already full and Joe's had to send out for more bottles.'

'Is Candy in?'

'Yes. She came in with Mr White.'

Anders smiled. 'Come to spend his winnings, I expect.'

The narrow stairs were uncarpeted and uneven but they were familiar, and Anders walked down slowly to the main club room. It held twenty-one tables with a bar along the length of one wall and in the corner was a dais that held the piano and its stool. It was a small Bechstein grand. The Bechstein had been the only way to bribe and keep Baldy Morton, the black American who plied his solitary, unheeded talent night after night. He loved the Bechstein, and that, and the fact that he hadn't got a work permit, were the reasons why he first came to the club. By now it was more than that. He liked Tad Anders, who appreciated his talent.

The air was heavy with cigar smoke, and the barman and the two girls were edging their way busily between tables with trays of glasses and empty bottles. The club members had the usual things in common. Few of them earned their livings honestly and most of them had plenty of money. And most of them were happy extroverts who spent their money freely on booze and girls. That was why they came to the club. There were at least half a dozen who had done break-ins for Tad at unlikely places for not much more than his goodwill. Admittedly, they would have been horrified if they had known they were unwittingly helping SIS. He got on well with most of them. They were ruthless and hard in their crimes but generous with their families and friends. The next day was a public holiday and the club would be virtually empty. The underworld treated holidays with proper respect, and they'd all be in their beds with their wives or other people's wives. Or walking around deserted buildings with nylon stockings over their faces, trying to remember where the Wages Office had been on the sketch done by one of the charladies.

Anders played his ration of being 'mine host', wandering from table to table, chatting with those he knew well, and exchanging an amiable nod with those he didn't recognise. And in the far corner was Candy Price, on her own, laughing at the mildly obscene references to her figure from the four men at the next table. He pulled up a chair and sat down facing her.

'Where's Chalky?'

'Gone to the loo.'

'How's your ma?'

'Same as usual. Up and down. How're you?'

'Same as your ma, up and down.'

'I hear madam was here tonight. She put you down as usual?'

He offered her a cigarette and leaned forward to light it for her and then leaned back and lit his own. She put her knee against his under the table. Candy came from Bethnal Green. Eighteen years old, blonde and pretty, with a figure that had been known to cause street accidents. She smiled across at him, not put off by his lack of response to her question.

'What d'you want me to say to Chalky?'

'About what?'

'Don't be stupid, lovie. Do I go back with him to his place or do you want me to stay the night?'

'What do *you* want to do?'

'I don't need the bread.'

'So?'

'So I'd rather stay with you.'

Candy Price had fallen for Tad Anders the first time she had seen him. It was serious and for real, and she showed her affection in the only ways she knew. She slept with him without payment and she bought him small presents. Sometimes a packet of Stuyvesants, sometimes a tie or a shirt that had taken her eye. Anders looked back at the big blue eyes that were watching his face. For once she wasn't all smiles.

'How about you stay the night and we go down to the coast tomorrow? We could take your old lady if you want.'

She reached across and touched his hand.

'I love you, Tad. I love you so much.'

'How are you going to deal with Chalky?'

She shrugged. 'God knows. He won't be a problem. He's half cut already.'

'Give me a ring on the bar phone when you're free.'

'OK.'

He stood up, took a last look around the room and then walked along the narrow corridor, past the toilets to the far stairs that took him up to his own living quarters and the two offices. The back office had a heavy steel door behind the wooden door and a complex locking device. The contrast with the rest of the club was extreme. The walls were panelled with rosewood, and the armchairs and three-seater settee were in soft tan leather. Good reproductions of French Impressionists were framed on three walls and the long wall was completely shelved from end to end. The upper shelves were packed with books and on the lowest shelf was a Technics hi-fi system and racks of cassettes. There were two digital GPO telephones and a red internal telephone. On the narrow wall beside the right-hand window was a photograph of a girl, a blonde. She was very beautiful, and she was smiling into the camera. A gentle, loving smile. Across the bottom right-hand corner, in a large feminine scrawl, it said *'Je t'aime infiniment – ta Marie-Claire.'* Tad Anders only looked at that photograph when he was depressed. Not because it cheered him up, but it gave him a logical reason for any inexplicable lowering of his spirits.

As he poured himself a whisky he turned on the hi-fi and the chimes of Big Ben rang out to herald the midnight news bulletin. He turned it off impatiently and he could hear the dull roar of the traffic in the Charing Cross Road.

He was asleep on the leather settee when the telephone rang. It was Candy Price and she was waiting for him downstairs. It was three-fifteen.

She was leaning over the piano in the deserted club and Baldy was playing softly and slowly, singing the words in his thin negro voice, and the girl with her chin cupped in her hands was listening intently. It was the melody she always asked for – 'Gettin' sentimental over you'. When his hands left the keys he looked up smiling at Anders.

'I still got the Dorsey version of that.'

The girl looked at the two men. From one face to the other. She wished she could have had brothers like them. Or even a father.

'Play Tad's tune for him, Baldy. The French one he likes.'

The negro looked up at Anders' face because he knew what the song meant for him. When Anders shrugged and nodded the negro played, and the second time around he came in at the end. '. . . *le temps passe et cours en battant tristement dans mon coeur si lourd . . . et pourtant, j'attendrai ton retour.'* Then very gently he closed the lid of the piano and stood up.

'Time for us chickens to roost, boss. See you day after tomorrow.'

'Night, Baldy. Take care.'

Anders and the girl sat on the beach on a damp, striped bath towel, and the old lady sat in a deckchair. They had lunched at a small restaurant in the High Street in Battle, on their way through to Bexhill. Candy's mother wasn't old, she was only fifty next October, but her body was grossly misshapen by arthritis. In spite of her bent back and her distorted hands and legs she was a cheerful woman whose life in the East End of London had inured her to the inevitable burdens that were the lot of the poverty-stricken generation that had grown up before and during the war. Uncomplaining despite the chronic pain, she was a good judge of people although she seldom aired her views. She liked Tad Anders.

Although she had never been told outright how her daughter earned a living she had a good idea of what went on. She was neither approving nor shocked. The girl was too pretty not to be a target for men. It had been like that when Candy was still at school. But Tad Anders was almost like a son. Easy-going, cheerful, protective, he was genuinely caring, and God knows there was no need to ingratiate himself with her in order to sleep with her daughter. She was used to Italians and East-End Jews and Tad Anders was very like them. A loner, who knew what he wanted and who took time to watch life going by. Her girl would come to no harm with this man, and that was more than she could say about most of them. She didn't see him as a husband; not because he was unavailable, but because girls who lived the kind of life that Candy lived always went on a few years too long, until they could no longer pick and choose. She had seen it all before, but there was no point in talking about it. When you are young and pretty, and the men are like bees round a honey pot, you can't believe that it could ever end.

Candy Price, in a white bikini, sat humming quietly to herself as she painted her toenails in Shocking Pink. When she had finished the paint job she fanned her toes with the *Daily Mail* until the lacquer had set hard. Then she sighed contentedly and lay back on the towel.

Anders sat looking across the beach out to sea where a long low tanker barely moved on the horizon; a Royal Navy frigate lay hull-down a mile or so behind the tanker. And when they had been up on the promenade he'd seen the long, thin grey smudge that was the coast of France. He had turned his eyes away deliberately because everything French reminded him of Marie-Claire Foubert and the nightmare in the dark, on the banks of the Thames at Marlow. It was years ago now, but it had been the end of a piece of his life when the Russians had thrown her bruised and battered body into the river. He had been standing under the tree in the moonlight, his hand on the Russian's throat as he made him talk, when he learned that it was too late and the girl was already dead. And beside himself with grief and rage, he had hunted Rudenko until he had him cornered in the churchyard. Mac had led him away and the doctor had given him an injection.

It had been two days and nights before he came to in his bed, and Mac had been sitting there, solemn-faced and concerned. And it had been Mac who told him that he was being taken off the SIS establishment and given the under-cover option. They had suggested a club as his cover and they had been generous with money. When he had asked why he was being dismissed Mac had sighed and asked if he didn't really already know. When he swore that he didn't, Mac had looked at his face for a long time before he spoke, and then he had told him that even though his shots had gone home, and Rudenko was dying, Anders had carved a great slit in his belly and pulled out his guts onto the damp night grass. There would be no enquiry and no comeback, but he was definitely out. SIS were not unused to violence but his kind of violence was politically dangerous. They would use it when it was necessary, but he was no longer part of the apparatus of the house in Queen Anne's Gate. He didn't remember doing it but Mac was a friend who had no reason to lie. And he said he had seen it, and taken quick action to protect both Anders and SIS. He had still been in coma when they buried Marie-Claire in the same churchyard of All Saints, and for almost two years his devil had frequently driven him in despair to the churchyard in Marlow to look at her grave. It was a ritual that gave him no peace or consolation. He drove down in reckless haste, parked the car by the church, walked into the churchyard and stared transfixed at the river. It was only when he eventually realised that he never actually looked at her grave that he stopped the frantic, neurotic journeys.

Anders had made no protest at their decision, and had accepted the option they offered. His life with SIS was all he knew. But he always considered they had been unfair. Marie-Claire was his girl, and Rudenko had let his men rape her before they killed her and threw her body in the river. It had been a piece of cold, deliberate revenge against him by Rudenko when he saw his operation falling apart. That surely made the circumstances different and unusual, but even Mac hadn't hesitated in going along with their decision. He was useful but dangerous, and that was the end of it for them. But they showed no embarrassment when they briefed him to do the things that went against their grain, and they took it for granted that he himself had no such scruples. He sensed that they no longer even considered him to be an Englishman. He was a Pole, their Slav, to counter the other Slavs from Dzerdzhinski Square.

He turned to look at the girl's face and even though her eyes were closed she said, 'What is it, Tad?'

'Nothing. I was just looking at you.'

She struggled up onto one elbow and half closed her eyes against the sun as she looked at his face.

'Are you OK?'

'I'm fine. How about you?'

'Another half-hour and we'll head back, yes?'

'Whatever you say, sweetie.'

He had taken a round-about route along narrow country lanes to get to Battle and he had glanced briefly at the old thatched cottage as he passed. There was blossom on the apple trees and it looked calm and welcoming with the orange light of the setting sun on the diamond-paned windows. He was sure that the girl hadn't noticed him looking.

Chapter 2

Although it was only the first week in September, Radio Moscow's weather bulletin that morning had reported that there had been light falls of snow during the night in Leningrad and warned of possible snowfalls in Moscow by that evening.

There were only six people sitting in the chairs facing the man standing at the lectern. He was not tall, but his dark eyes dominated his face and his audience. He was leaning with his arms on the old wooden lectern as he looked at them all intently. His voice was soft and educated with a faint trace of a Leningrad accent. He pushed aside the light on its swivel so that he could lean further forward, as if the few extra inches might make a difference.

'. . . and one last thing I want to say to you. Go search for people who are hurt by fate or nature – the ugly, those suffering from an inferiority complex, craving power and influence but defeated by unfavourable circumstances . . . The sense of belonging to an influential, powerful organisation will give them a feeling of superiority over the handsome and prosperous people around them. For the first time in their lives they will experience a sense of importance . . . It is sad indeed, and humanly shallow – but we are obliged to profit from it.'

There was a long silence as his dark eyes scanned their faces, and then he stood up straight. He nodded towards them. 'Goodnight, comrades.' And there was a clatter of feet as they all stood up as he walked to the door and left the room. General Pavl Anatolevich Sudotplatov was the commander of *Spetsburo* Number One: the KGB's special unit entrusted with peacetime sabotage and murder. His audience had just completed their final three years' training as field operatives for whichever Soviet Intelligence service might choose to use them. At least one would go to the Red Army's Intelligence service, the GRU; one would probably operate under the direct control of the Politburo; and the others would stay with the newly founded KGB. All of them were already commissioned officers. They had another week of final indoctrination when they would be shown what were some of the most closely guarded secrets of the Soviet Union.

They were given only fifteen minutes in the laboratory known as the *Kamera*, whose staff spent their time and hundreds of thousands of roubles perfecting methods of killing human beings by devices and poisons that had no antidotes, and left no traces in the victim's body. Their short transit through the laboratory required the students to walk between chalked guide-lines to prevent them accidentally touching some innocent-looking lethal artefact. There were few official visitors to the *Kamera*. Even inside the Politburo which authorised it, and the KGB who operated it and used its research, it was feared rather than respected.

Vasili Pavlovich Burinski was one of the group who ended up on the KGB's payroll. He had been trained at three KGB schools with all their normal thoroughness. Apart from his intelligence training he spoke fluent German and good English. His father had been a full colonel in the Red Army, a career officer who had commanded an artillery regiment that had helped to defend Moscow, and fired the first barrage into beleaguered Berlin. He had lost an arm and an eye in the last week before the city fell and had been promoted to Major General. His wife had been killed in the siege of Leningrad and he now had a small government apartment in the centre of Moscow and a *dacha* in the pine woods just off the Volokolamskoye Highway beyond the Arkhangelskoye Estate. With no interest in politics, his only interest in life had been the educating and bringing up of his only child. When his son had left Moscow University and had been chosen for training at the Frunze Academy he had been lonely, but happy that his son would follow in his military footsteps. When Vasili had been transferred to the KGB he hid his anger and disappointment. If you were a career officer in the Red Army you needed to be a committed Soviet to find virtue in the KGB. If you were not so committed you despised and subconsciously feared them. General Burinski kept his views to himself but his anger came from the fact that it was the first time in their lives that his son and he had a subject they studiously avoided. His disappointment showed only in his never enquiring about his son's work or his progress. His love and concern were as obvious as they had always been but the talk was always of chess and books and the countryside.

Burinski was the only one of the new intake who was taken back to the *Kamera* again. There was a long row of offices in the compound, away from the main building, and it was there that he was interviewed.

The man who interviewed him was a short, thickset KGB man in his late fifties. Burinski recognised the type. A committed Soviet who had survived from the days of the OGPU, the NKVD and all the other upheavals that finally produced the KGB. Dedicated and experienced, they carried out their orders with unquestioning obedience. Burinski saw the file on the desk with his own name stencilled on the front. It was thicker than he expected and he wondered what it could contain to be so full.

'And how is your father, comrade Burinski?'

'I haven't seen him for three months, comrade Major, but he seems well enough from his letters.'

'A pity he never joined the Party.'

'He's not interested in politics. The Red Army was always the whole of his life.'

'And you? What are your interests?'

'My work.'

Karpov nodded, not so much in approval as a sign that

he recognised the correct and standard response to his question.

'It's been suggested that you are capable of carrying out special tasks for the *Spetsburo*. What do you think?'

'I'll do whatever the Bureau orders me to do.'

Karpov half-smiled and leaned back in his chair.

'Easy to say, young man. I've heard people make that sort of rash statement before, and then when they're told what they have to do they back down.'

He waited for the younger man to answer, but he sat there in silence, his blue eyes arrogant and challenging. Karpov reached for a file from a metal trolley behind him.

'There is a man named Krause. Doctor Emil Krause. He's a judge of the West Berlin High Court. A fanatical anti-Soviet who has handed out long terms of imprisonment to some of our people who have been trapped over there. We'd like you to bring him back into East Berlin so that we can talk with him.' He slid the file across his desk to Burinski. 'Read it and come back with a plan, tomorrow.'

Burinski reached for the file, and Karpov said, 'It doesn't go outside the compound, my friend. There's a room put aside for you in Block F.'

Burinski's plan had been approved and he had spent two weeks in East Berlin, crossing several times into West Berlin, checking Krause's movements and a route back to the Wall. In the third week Burinski and a KGB man from Karlshorst had stopped Krause in the street, and in open daylight they had bundled him into a black Mercedes on the Kurfürstendamm and driven straight to the Brandenburger Tor. The barrier opened to let them through, and then closed behind them. Krause had been flown to Moscow in a military plane the same night.

The American and British commanders jointly protested vigorously against the kidnapping to the Soviet authorities who indignantly denied any knowledge of Dr Krause or his abduction. It was nearly five years later when the Soviet Red

Cross announced the death of Dr Krause in an unnamed Soviet prison. It was a piece of outrageous impudence that expressed the mounting arrogance of the men in the Kremlin.

Burinski's next two assignments were both kidnappings. One in Vienna, and the other, more complex, in Paris. The abduction in Paris had required the use of one of the *Kamera*'s special drugs.

After three years he was posted to East Berlin, and his new operations were more precise. The targets were defectors from the Eastern bloc countries and leading anti-Communist figures in West Germany as well as West Berlin. And they were to be killed, not kidnapped. He had had special training at the *Kamera* laboratories on their secret murder weapons. Weapons that left no trace of killing. No wounds, no blood, no medical symptoms even after an autopsy. And the weapons themselves were not like weapons but cigarette cases, a toothpaste tube and sometimes merely a tablet or a powder.

They had shown Burinski a light metal tube that looked like a cigar container, and a sectional drawing showing how the device worked. Then they told him about blood vessels, with slides on a screen of normal blood vessels and the contracted blood vessels of a woman who had died of a heart attack, and they explained about the gas and the antidote pill.

The instructor and one of the scientists drove out with him to the nearby woods. The big German Shepherd was on a chain. At the woods they gave him the antidote pill and watched him slip it into his mouth. They warned him again that it worked very quickly. Less than fifteen seconds, and its effects only lasted three minutes. The dog was chained to a tree and it wagged its tail as he approached. Two feet away from the dog he pressed the button on the steel tube and heard the glass ampoule shatter as it was struck by the needle. There was no other sound and for a moment he thought the device had failed. Then the dog shuddered terribly, its legs gave, and for a few seconds it convulsed silently, its paws frantically scattering the fallen leaves. In less than thirty seconds it was dead. Coldly and precisely the scientist explained once again how the weapon caused all the body's blood vessels to contract, instantly stopping the heart. But in ten minutes, as the effects of the drug wore off, the vessels would dilate again and even the most rigorous autopsy would diagnose that death was caused by a heart attack. The diagnosis would be correct and there would be no evidence to indicate that it was prussic acid vapour that had induced the attack.

Burinski walked back slowly to the car. He felt faint, but was determined not to show that he had been affected in even the slightest way by the demonstration. But he remembered the green moss and lichen on the weather side of the tree and the red of the fallen leaves. And the fact that every part of the dog had quivered while it was dying, its muzzle and neck, its chest and belly, and the long muscles in its haunches and hind legs had rippled as if they were liquid. For the first time he realised why even the top men feared the *Spetsburo*. He feared them now himself. What had happened to the dog could happen to him.

Burinski watched Yushenko every day for nearly three weeks. The defector had got himself a job as a repair mechanic for a typewriter company in Cologne. The West Germans had given him a new name and new documents but Moscow had identified him long before they sent in Burinski. He lived in a small flat in an inexpensive block off Salzgasse and led a quiet, regular life. He left for work every morning at 7.30 and spent the day in the workshop, eating sandwiches and reading the daily paper at his lunch-time break. At 5 p.m. he left promptly, bought a packet of American cigarettes and groceries at a neighbourhood shop and was home by 5.30.

The exception to this routine was Friday nights, when Yushenko left his flat as soon as it was dark and walked up to the Hohenzollernring, where he picked up one of the girls and went home with her. In the three weeks that Burinski had been watching it was always a different girl, but they were always girls who had a place nearby. Yushenko would stay for an hour and then walk back to his flat.

It was nine o'clock when Yushenko walked out of the building and made his way through the side streets to the St Apostoln church and then past the museum to Rudolfplatz. There were no girls there when Yushenko arrived and he looked at his watch and walked slowly down Hohenzollernring towards the savings bank building. There were two girls by the carpet shop and Yushenko spoke to one of them, and a few moments later they walked off together. As they stood at the edge of the pavement Burinski thought for a horrible moment that they were going to take a taxi, but they were only waiting for cars to pass so that they could cross the wide street. He watched them enter Lindenstrasse and then followed them. Down one of the side streets the girl stopped at a newspaper shop, and using a key she let them both in to a narrow passageway that led to a flight of stairs. He saw the light go on behind the curtains of the second floor window and settled down to wait.

There was no traffic in the narrow street, but a few pedestrians meant that he had to move on from time to time, looking in the unlit shop windows without straying too far. He was actually level with the newspaper shop when Yushenko eventually came out and Burinski crossed the narrow street towards him. Yushenko was lighting a cigarette and Burinski took out his cigarettes as he went up to him and asked for a light. In the flare of the lighter Burinski saw that Yushenko's face was deeply lined and his skin covered with a rash. As his cigarette glowed he gripped the tube in his jacket pocket and took it out as he slid the tablet into his mouth. He said very softly '*Spasiba, tovarich Yushenko.*' He saw the look of horror on Yushenko's face then he lifted the tube and pressed the button. The effect was immediate, the defector's hands went to his chest as he collapsed in the shop doorway, and as Burinski walked away he heard the man's shoes scrabbling frenziedly on the paving stones. It made him think for a moment of dry autumn leaves, and lichen on the trunk of a tree.

Burinski phoned the safe-house from the car park on the Ring road and they drove him to the airport at Wahn where he was given a ticket for the internal flight to West Berlin that left an hour later. He wondered if he dared telephone Inge to meet him. He decided against it. They probably monitored all calls to East Berlin automatically.

It was past midnight when he landed at Berlin but there was a KGB car waiting for him. He phoned Inge before he left the airport. She sounded pleased to hear from him and said she would get a bath and a meal ready for him. Her flat was only ten minutes walk from his headquarters in Lichtenburg.

Karpov was waiting for him. He was a Lieutenant-Colonel now, and he had flown in from Moscow especially to see Burinski. He was obviously pleased with Burinski's mission. It seemed that Moscow were pleased too. Karpov brought confirmation of Burinski's promotion to captain. He reported what had happened but Karpov obviously already knew. Bonn had already lodged an angry protest with Moscow who had routinely denied all knowledge of the affair. There was little to say as they sat drinking their coffee.

'D'you want a driver to take you home?'

'No thanks. I'll walk.'

'It's a long walk to your place, my boy.'

For a moment he hesitated, and then he said, 'I'm making a call first.'

'Who is it? The dark-haired girl?'

'Yes.'

'Why not a nice Soviet girl? There's plenty of pretty ones here at Karlshorst. Why pick a German?'

Burinski shrugged. 'I didn't pick her for her nationality, comrade Colonel. I find her attractive, and pleasant company.'

'She's a German, comrade. Don't trust her. Don't risk a promising career for a pretty face and a pair of big tits. We can find you plenty of those in Moscow.'

Karpov stood up and held out his hand, and as Burinski took it Karpov said, 'But at least she provides good background for your cover as an East German.'

As Burinski walked slowly through the deserted streets he knew that he must have been under surveillance all the time since he had been in East Berlin. He took it for granted that there would have been routine checks: KGB officers were as suspect as anyone else, maybe more. Were they really warning him off, or just being their usual bloody-minded selves where all foreigners were concerned? The German Democratic Republic might be the Soviet Union's most important ally but it didn't make Moscow like Germans, wherever they came from.

Inge was smiling as she opened the door and she was wearing a white frothy *peignoir*. She must have been asleep before he called from the airport but she had made up her face and looked sleepily glamorous.

They kissed passionately, and ten minutes later he was lying back in the warm bath as she made him an omelette. Before drying himself he slid on his bathrobe, walked back into the living room and took the small parcel from his plastic Scandinavian Airline's bag. He walked into the kitchen and put the package on the table.

'Something from Paris for you.'

He was amused at her excitement as she eagerly tore off the flowered paper. It was a small phial of Chanel No. 5, and she was delighted.

Chapter 3

INGE LAUFER worked as a secretary at the offices of the East German Press Service. She wasn't a member of the Party, but nobody cared too much about the political leanings of secretaries and typists. But two days after Burinski had come back she was called to the office of the Editor-in-Chief.

She had never been in his office before. It was large and modern with two TV sets, a radio, a tape-recorder and a Telex. He was a burly man with grey hair and she had heard that he'd been a Party member since before the war. He waved her to a chair in front of his desk.

'Fraülein Laufer?'

'Yes, sir.'

'How long have you been working for us?'

'Three years six months.'

'Do you like your work?'

'Yes.'

'You're working for the news desk, yes?'

'Yes, sir.'

'There's a possibility of promotion as secretary to the News Editor himself. Are you interested?'

'Yes, of course.'

'It's a career post, you understand. Not a job.'

'I don't understand.'

'Your work would have to take precedence over everything else. Over your social life for instance.'

'My social life is very limited already, Herr Lemke.'

But she knew now where they were heading.

'So I understand. But you'd be willing to forgo these outside . . . relationships and concentrate on your work here.'

'I'm afraid not.'

'You're not interested in the promotion, then?'

'Oh yes, I'm interested, but not at that price.'
'Is the relationship that important to you?'
'I think so.'
'You aren't sure?'
'He's asked me to marry him. I haven't answered him.'
'You know what he does?'
'He works for the Ministry of the Interior.'
'What as?'
'I've no idea.'
He sighed and leaned back in his chair.
'Fraülein Laufer, you surely don't need me to put it more bluntly, but you would be wise to drop this relationship. Not crudely or suddenly. You're an attractive young girl. You must have had such situations before. Suitors who don't interest you, and you gently put them to one side. You could be tactful. Just let it fade quietly away.'
She smiled. 'You flatter me, Herr Lemke. With five women to every man what you describe doesn't happen in the Democratic Republic.'
'So?'
'So if I have to choose between the man and the promotion I should choose the man.'
'Well. At least we know where we stand. Thank you.'
'So no promotion?' she said as she stood up.
'I'll think about it.'
She walked back slowly to her desk in the newsroom, angry and disturbed. Who the hell did they think they were, deciding every aspect of everybody's life? And doing it so blandly, as if they took obedience for granted. You didn't just carry out orders, you were expected to obey even vague hints. It was bad enough that the Russians lived in their cloud-cuckoo land, but what she couldn't understand was how Germans like Lemke could go along with it. He wasn't uninformed, he saw uncensored news items from all over the world, but he was still willing to send out the clap-trap that went for news items, as if he thought they would be believed. Not even the East German public believed them. They heard the real news on their radios. So who did they think they were

deceiving? Even the Russian public took the official news with a pinch of salt. Did the Party really think that because the Allies had drawn a line on a map and divided Germany in two that half the Germans had lost the power to think? She never discussed politics with Burinski but she knew from some of the things he said that he followed the Party line. He must be more important than he made out, and working for the Ministry of the Interior could cover anything from controlling the price of vegetables to the police. And she'd noticed the small printed label on the bottom of the Chanel No. 5 that said it was bought at the duty free shop at Wahn airport, not Paris. He hadn't actually said that he had bought it in Paris. She remembered the words – 'Something from Paris for you.' And it *was* from Paris originally. Not a lie, but not the truth.

Chapter 4

BURINSKI TOOK three days of his accumulated leave, Inge was on leave from the Friday night, and they borrowed a car and drove down to the Harz mountains, to Wernigerode.

The German Democratic Republic, East Germany, is a small country – about half the size of the State of Oregon, or half the size of Great Britain, according to viewpoint. Twenty-five kilometres from the centre of Berlin, and the harsh realities of the Wall and the rival powers of occupation, the landscape changes to a countryside of quiet plains and thickly-forested mountains. Mainly rural and, like farming all over the world, only obliquely touched by occupying forces or even wars, the majority of its people had no wish to cross the barbed-wire frontiers. They lived their lives indifferent to governments and decrees and ideologies, much more concerned with weather and good husbandry. They worked hard and had nothing to fear. They no more thought of joining the Communist Party than they had the Nationalist Socialist Party of Adolf Hitler. They were not enthusiasts about anything, not even the Soviet Union's hybrid wheats and barleys that were claimed to crop forty per cent heavier than traditional strains.

It was against this background that Inge Laufer grew up. A farmer's daughter, she could milk a cow, harness a plough-horse, drive a tractor and bake bread. She had completed all but the last half-year at the Hochschule in Weimar. That was when the Russians had come. Her father farmed two hundred acres, and as the Russians settled into the city there had been talk of breaking up the farms into fifty-acre holdings, but it never came to anything. The Russians needed all the foodstuffs they could get, and apart from a few hot-heads and sycophants there had been no local clamour to take farms over.

The phone was ringing as Anders opened the door to his flat. It was Peter Nicholson.

'Tad, I've just had a phone call from one of our chaps. I've told him to come straight to you. He's in trouble—bleeding quite a bit—should be with you in a few minutes. His name's Mason. Jerry Mason. Will you look after him until I get there? I'll bring a doctor as soon as I can lay hands on one . . . OK?'

'What's he look like?'

'Young, dark hair, Zapata moustache. I must go.'

'See you.'

Anders hung up and walked down the stairs, along the corridor and up the stairs to the reception area. He switched on the light and opened the double door. A man was sitting on one of the dustbins, one arm hugging his chest, his head back against the brick wall. He had dark hair and a moustache. Anders walked forward and stood in front of the man.

'What's the matter?'

'Find Anders . . . at the club . . . please.'

'I'm Anders.'

'Nicholson said . . .' The man tried to suppress a thin cry of pain and failed. Anders put his own hand on the back of the man's hand where it was pressed to his side inside his sports jacket. The man's hand was wet and warm and slippery with blood. Anders slid one hand under the man's knees and put his arm round his shoulders. The man was heavier than he expected and inside the reception area he rested him for a moment on the desk as he kicked the door to behind him.

The man was unconscious as Anders lowered him gently on to his leather couch. With scissors from the kitchen he sliced off half the man's jacket and then his shirt. Gently shifting the man's hand he saw the wound. The slug had hit the bottom rib and sliced across the soft flesh of his belly to leave a six-inch long flap of loose flesh that was seeping blood. Anders propped the man up against two cushions and covered the wound with a towel soaked in cold water. A few minutes later he heard the bell ringing downstairs.

Nicholson had a tall gangling man with him in evening dress and as he led them along the corridor to the stairs and his room Nicholson said, 'How bad is he, Tad?'

'Fair amount of blood lost. I'd say he's in shock.'

Anders and Nicholson stood in silence as they watched the doctor lift off the sopping wet towel and peer at the wound. He checked the wounded man's pulse with his wristwatch and then stood up.

'It wasn't a bullet. Somebody struck him with a knife. Hit his rib and it slid downwards and across his abdomen, slicing open the skin . . . looks as if he might have lost up to half a pint of blood.'

'What does he need?' asked Nicholson.

'He needs to go into hospital . . . needs some blood, a thorough check and some sewing up. I don't think anything vital has been touched but we'll soon find out.'

Nicholson shook his head. 'He can't go into a general ward.'

'I'll take him to my place in Welbeck Street. But he'll need some blood first and some temporary patching up. We can't move him as he is.'

Nicholson looked worried. 'We'll have to put a guard on him while he's with you.'

'That's no problem. We usually have that with your people.'

'Can you fix it now and get the blood over? He's 'O' group.'

The doctor turned towards Anders. 'Can I use your phone?'

Anders nodded. 'The one on the left. The grey one. Just dial.'

Fifteen minutes later two medical orderlies slid the unconscious man on to a stretcher and Nicholson and the doctor followed Anders to the waiting private ambulance. The doctor climbed in with the wounded man.

The first light of the false dawn was already stirring the pigeons, and empty vans from the Home Counties were heading for the markets. It looked as if it were going to be a very hot day.

Anders made coffee for himself and Nicholson and they sat together in the small bright kitchen.

'What had your chap Mason been up to, Peter?'

'He's been checking on an Armenian named Kanassian. He's got a warehouse on the river at Blackfriars. Buys and sells oriental carpets. High-class stuff, and genuine, but we had a quiet look at his bank balances. There's not much there and we think he's a banker for the KGB. They provide the carpets. He sells them, and the money goes to fund KGB operations here.'

'What happened last night?'

'A month ago we established a positive link between the Soviet Embassy and Kanassian. We discovered a KGB dead-letter box. They were using a loose coping stone on the embankment near the Festival Hall. Kanassian was seen using it. We didn't pick him up but we checked the package he had left. It was a newspaper cutting . . . just a couple of inches of a single column with the racing results from Sandown Park. And – of course – a microdot. The microdot gave details of cash deposits in lockers at the main London railway stations. We left everything as it was but it was decided that we'd have a look at Kanassian's warehouse and his living quarters. He lives there too. That's what Mason was doing last night. I don't know what happened but he phoned me from a call-box by Leicester Square underground station. I sent him round to you.'

'Why so much secrecy now?'

Nicholson shrugged. 'We didn't have a warrant and we want to find out what happened before we take any action.'

'Did he go alone?'

'Yes.'

Anders raised his eyebrows. 'You guys never learn, do you?'

'What's that mean?'

'It's crazy sending out one man when you already know the KGB are involved. It needs a proper set-up. A full recce, radio support and a back-up team. You've blown Mason. And you've closed down their operation when you'd have got far more just letting it run until you'd got it fully evaluated. You could probably have turned Kanassian and used him.'

'I doubt it.'

'How much money was there in the lockers?'

'Just over seventy thousand.'

'Dollars or pounds?'

'Pounds.'

'Have you collared it?'

'They're doing that now.'

'And Kanassian?'

'We'll deport him when we know from Mason what went on.'

'Why don't you knock him off? Teach them a lesson.'

'Is it justified?'

'Oh for Christ's sake, Peter. Anything's justified with those bastards.'

'Would you do it yourself?'

'Sure. Providing you ask me to.'

'Maybe we will. Let's wait until I can talk with Mason.'

And that was how they left it.

Burinski booked two rooms in a small inn at the edge of the town and they lazed the days away. It was on the second day, when they were sitting at the edge of the forest looking over the quiet valley that she told him of the pressures at her office.

He smiled and shrugged. 'They did the same to me.'

'Why are they doing it? Why do we matter so much?'

He turned to look at her. She was very beautiful and her big brown eyes were clear and honest.

'Have you decided yet?'

'Decided what?' She smiled.

'Don't tease. You know what I mean.'

'Do you still want to marry me?'

'You know I do.'

'They might try and stop us.'

He shrugged. 'They'll try, maybe, but they won't refuse in the end.'

She looked at his face, intently. 'Who are the "they" we're talking about?'

'Your bosses and mine.'

'Herr Lemke couldn't give a damn who I marry. It will have come from your people at the Ministry.'

'You're probably right.' He smiled at her and said softly, 'So what's your answer?'

She looked away from him, gazing over the valley, touching a limp stem of red campion to her mouth. Without turning to look at him she said, 'The answer's yes; if you're sure that's what you want.'

He reached out for her hand. 'When?'

She laughed gently and looked at him. 'Whenever you want.'

He stood up and pulled her up alongside him. He turned her, kissing her gently, her body against his, warm and soft.

'I'll start things moving as soon as we get back to Berlin.'

And suddenly the mere name of the city was grim and grey and menacing.

After they had made love in her bed that night he had gone back to his own room next door. He pulled up a chair to the small window, lit a cigarette and looked out. He could see the outline of the pine trees in the light of the moon, and he wished that he could stay there for the rest of his life. He knew he'd have to tell her before they actually got married, and she would know he had lied. Lied about almost everything, except that he loved her. She wouldn't believe that he only lied because it was his duty to lie. His duty to his calling, and his duty to his country. She never recognised such loyalties.

She wasn't committed as he was. Tomorrow was their last full day. He would tell her tomorrow. He looked at his watch. It was one o'clock. Tomorrow was already today.

He put if off again and again. Hoping to find the right opening that would lead to it naturally. But no such opening came. They visited the museum in the morning, and in the afternoon they walked again to the place where they had sat the previous day. She seemed so happy, and so sure that they were both going to be happy. And she insisted on gathering a bag of the big pine cones to take back with them. She said they were good weather guides. She was counting them, moving them from the heap beside her into the red canvas bag.

Eventually she turned, smiling. 'Fifty-seven.'

'Are you warm enough here?'

'Yes, of course I am. And I've got a sweater in my bag. What about you?'

'Will you listen very carefully?' And his voice trembled. 'I've got something I want to tell you.'

'You sound very solemn all of a sudden,' she said softly.

He looked away from her face, focusing his eyes on the red canvas bag.

'I'm not German, Inge. I'm a Russian. And I'm a captain in the KGB.'

Compelled to see her reaction he looked back to her face. She had closed her eyes as if she had received a blow and when she opened them she sighed before she spoke. And tears rimmed her eyes.

'They won't let us marry. They'll just send you back to Moscow.'

'But what about you?'

'What do you mean?'

'Are you disappointed that I'm a Russian?'

She looked at him calmly. 'I never loved you because you were German. That just doesn't matter.'

'What does matter?'

'They pressured both of us. But it was only a nudge compared with what they'll do when you tell them you want to marry me.'

'But if they don't object, you'd still marry me?'

'I fell in love with a man. It makes no difference to me whether you're German, Russian or Chinese. You're just you as far as I'm concerned.'

'What about the other thing?'

She smiled. 'You mean the KGB?'

'Yes.'

'If you like playing cowboys and Indians that's up to you.'

'It's more than that, Inge, my work . . .'

She held up her hand to silence him. 'I don't want to hear. Whatever you do you must feel that it's right to do it. That's enough for me.'

'You really mean that?'

'Of course.'

'You're very generous. You haven't pointed out that I told you a pack of lies.'

'Moscow lives on lies. How could you be different and survive?'

'For God's sake don't say anything like that if they talk to you about us marrying.'

She smiled. 'Are you afraid they might send me to the Gulag?'

'It's not a joke, Inge. The Gulag really does exist.'

She smiled. 'Hadn't you better tell me your name? Your real name?'

He sighed. 'It's terrible when I hear you say that.' He half-smiled, embarrassed. 'Maybe you won't like it.'

'Try me.'

'Vasili Pavlovich Burinski.'

He sounded defensive, and she leaned forward and kissed him gently.

'Vasili Pavlovich Burinski, I love you.'

He pulled her to him fiercely, and with his head resting on her shoulder he said, 'I love you so much, Inge. I was so worried about telling you, but you've made it so easy.'

She stroked his shoulder gently, soothing him as mothers soothe their children.

Karpov had flown in from Moscow the day after Burinski reported that he wanted to marry Inge Laufer. Karpov's attitude had ranged from the fatherly to the recriminating. From despair to barrack-room male chauvinism. There was probably nothing wrong with the girl, but why oh why marry a foreigner when there were millions, literally millions, of Russian girls to choose from? Girls who would be proud of his rank and the organisation he served. For that matter why marry at all, why load your shoulders with all that responsibility? Sow some wild oats by all means, but for God's sake you don't have to buy it outright. What he needed was a couple of weeks' leave in Moscow to remind himself of what pretty girls were like. Karpov himself would see that he had a special selection.

It wasn't an aggressive interview. There were no threats and Karpov didn't say that the marriage was impossible. He nagged and derided but he said nothing against the girl herself beyond the fact that she was a foreigner. They had obviously done a lot of checking on her but there was nothing in Karpov's harangue to indicate that anything negative had been discovered.

After they had lunched together Karpov had a private telephone conversation with Moscow, and when he sent for Burinski again the atmosphere was relaxed. Moscow, he said, were not too happy about his request. Apart from the fact that she was a foreigner the girl was not a Party member and seemed to have no political convictions at all. That was a dangerous vacuum in the background of the wife of a KGB officer. On the other hand Moscow wanted him to be content, and if this marriage was what he wanted they would agree, with certain provisos. He would never discuss his work with her. Not even a cover story. She would have to accept that his work was closed to her and she would not interfere in any way. Moscow would also arrange for her to see the Party at work in the Republic. She would visit various works and schools, hospitals and research laboratories so that she could absorb the efforts that were being made to make East Germany economically and socially advanced. It was also accepted that marrying her would give a genuine basis to Burinski's cover story of being an East German. Nevertheless, he would have to play his part. It would be up to him to help make her at least a supporter of the Party line if not an enthusiast. Burinski assured him that he would do everything possible to repay their faith in him.

There was no comment and no pressures on Inge at the office of the Presse Dienst but she was vaguely aware of glances in her direction by senior people who would normally have ignored her.

Ten days later, permission came through from Moscow for them to marry. Karpov broke the good news, hedged about again with warnings of dire consequences if the girl did not conform to accepted Party behaviour for Soviet officials' wives. They were allowed to marry in church in Inge's home village just outside Weimar and her parents were impressed by her young husband. They had a three-day honeymoon before they went back to East Berlin, where they were given privileged married quarters in a block that housed senior officials of the Red Army Intelligence Staff and the East Germans' Intelligence service, MfS.

The two Germans sat on one side of the table and Peter Nicholson on the other. The room was thick with smoke and Kiefer was lighting yet another cigarette. He threw the used match at the ashtray and missed, and left the match to smoke on the polished table top. Gierecke reached for it and put it in the tray. They had been talking for two hours; and the dead-lock was solid.

It was Kiefer who broke the silence. 'Would it help if we came to London, Herr Nicholson?'

'By all means. You'd be very welcome but it would make no difference. What you are asking puts it into the political field. It's no longer just a counter-intelligence matter. They couldn't possibly agree.'

Gierecke sighed. 'Our agreement was made a long time ago. Nearly ten years. Neither party could have foreseen a situation like this. Surely London must understand that?'

'There's every sympathy with your situation, but to extend the present arrangements could have all sorts of repercussions.'

'Meantime we just sit on our backsides while they send over professional assassins who are safely back over the border in a couple of hours.' Gierecke shook his head slowly. 'Bonn couldn't let this go on.'

Nicholson shrugged. 'That would be a question for the two governments to sort out.'

Kiefer lit another cigarette. 'Their people in East Berlin must be expecting some reaction, for God's sake.'

'That could be why they are doing this. Just to make us react. So that they have an excuse for another blockade of Berlin. Or something even more provocative. Imagine what a propaganda victory they would have if anything went wrong. West Germans being sent into East Berlin or East Germany as revenge killers? You would be totally exposed and isolated. The rest of Europe and the Americans couldn't possibly support you.'

Gierecke spoke very softly. 'So why don't you people look after it?'

Nicholson shook his head. 'There's no possibility of that. If something went wrong it could be catastrophic. They would really have an excuse to attack West Berlin. You've heard what Radio Moscow is saying already: West Berlin is being used as a base for the Americans and the British to launch their spies into the Democratic Republic. And if something goes wrong we've handed the proof to them on a silver salver. And whatever they did in West Berlin half the world would say we had got what we deserve and the other half would hold its breath and say nothing.'

'What do they have to do, Herr Nicholson, before we retaliate? Two more assassinations? Four? A member of the

West German cabinet? Where do you draw the line? Or can they just go on killing as they please?'

'We can put British Army units with your Frontier Police and we'll feed you all the information we get out of Moscow and Berlin that could help you deal with them when they come over.'

Kiefer smiled. A cold contemptuous smile. 'If you gave us the whole of the Rhine Army it would make no difference.'

Nicholson didn't rise to the bait. 'I suggest, gentlemen, that we report back to our chiefs and leave it to them to decide what to do.'

It was the soft-spoken Gierecke who said the words he had hoped he wouldn't hear. 'You won't expect our cooperation in Berlin from now onwards, will you?'

'Is that official?'

'Yes.'

'You're quite sure? If I pass that on it will hinder rather than help.'

'It's official, Herr Nicholson, make no mistake about that.'

'I assume your people discussed the implications of withdrawing cooperation with SIS?'

Gierecke nodded. 'Extensively.'

Nicholson sighed. 'May I ask at what level the discussion took place?'

'Top level BfV, and a representative from the Chancellor's office, the Foreign Ministry and the Opposition.' Gierecke paused. 'It's not a bluff, Herr Nicholson, I assure you.'

'I'll go back to London and report on our meeting. Would you be available for a further meeting at the end of the week?'

'We're available at any time.'

Back in London Nicholson reported to French.

'D'you think they mean it, Peter, about withdrawing cooperation?'

'I do.'

'Including Berlin?'

'Yes. They're very bitter about it. Gierecke drove me

back to the airport and he told me that it was possible that they would take unilateral action if we didn't do something about it.'

'D'you think they will?'

'I don't think so. But I wouldn't bet on it. I suspect they'll be letting off steam at Cabinet level before long.'

'They have already. The West German Ambassador had an hour with the Foreign Secretary late last night. There was no threat of going it alone, but they were very steamed up and the Minister was sympathetic but adamant.'

'They've got a good case. They haven't got a chance of picking up a trained professional who slips over the border after an unknown victim, kills and is back home an hour or two later. Whoever was facing the problem would have no choice. An eye for an eye. But they don't even have the choice. If they did it without our agreement or the American's they'd be out in the snow even if they were successful.'

Sir Arthur pursed his lips as he looked across his desk at Nicholson. 'What would you propose if, in the end, something had to be done?'

'We couldn't possibly let the Germans do it. It would have to be us. I can only think of one sensible solution.'

'Anders?'

'Yes.'

Chapter 5

FOR SEVEN or eight weeks Burinski was given desk work at the intelligence centre in Normannenstrasse and he and his wife were taken on escorted visits to schools, factories, trade-union meetings and government departments. Their escorts were always experts in the field concerned, who were able to explain and answer their questions. And comparisons were drawn with what was being done for the people in West Berlin and West Germany. Burinski was impressed and his wife made few comments and asked no questions.

When he tried to discuss the visits with her she wouldn't be drawn. She never disagreed with what he said but she never agreed either. She just listened, half-smiling, as he praised the benefits that the East Germans got from adopting the Soviet system. It was after a visit to a tyre plant that he provoked her into a reply. He didn't intend to provoke her; they were sitting together after their evening meal and he read out the production figures from the handouts they'd been given, and then he'd looked at her smiling.

'The same production as the Americans. Same output per man and with cheaper costs. Those are facts, Inge, not propaganda.'

'I'm sure you're right, Vasili.'

He smiled back at her. 'You don't believe it, do you?'

She shrugged. 'There's football on TV if you want it.'

'Why don't you believe, Inge?'

She sighed. 'There's no way of knowing whether the figures are true or phoney. And that isn't the point.'

'What is the point?'

'Those tyres all go to the Soviet Union. You'd have to get it on the black market if you wanted one and you were German. About a month's pay is the going rate.'

'Are you sure?'

She reached out and put her hand gently on his as it lay on the arm of his chair.

'We don't have to quarrel about things like this, Vasili. None of it matters.'

'But I want to know what you think.'

'Do you mean that? Really mean it?'

'Of course I do.'

'I'll tell you. Then let's not ever discuss these things again.'

'OK.'

She took a deep breath. 'Hitler started the war against the Soviet Union. We lost it, and now we're paying for it. In the first few months we paid the Red Army. They looted and raped and sent convoys back to Russia loaded with the loot. Everything you could imagine. Wooden doors, toilets, carpets, furniture, everything. No German old enough to remember is ever going to forget those days. Now it's all done officially. You use paper and forms to loot us now and there's no more raping of women. It's just factories and farms being raped now. We do as we're told because arguing can get you in jail. There is no freedom of speech, no democracy, no political opposition, and we're kept in East Berlin by the Wall. Maybe we deserve it, whether we do or not we've got it.'

'Does that mean you hate all Russians?'

'Of course it doesn't. I love *you*, and I've met many Russians I like. You've all got the same dictatorship that we have. The only difference is that the Russians never had anything better. But we did.'

'Is there nothing good that we've done in the Republic?'

'That's not the point, Vasili. We're an occupied country. And we're occupied by a dictatorship. The news is censored and distorted. We don't have news, we have propaganda. We can only hear the real news from other countries on our radios. We know our news is a pack of lies and we just have to pretend we've been fooled. It's all a pretence. We've *not* been fooled. We were once part of the real world and living in this . . . this deception, is degrading.'

'But before the Revolution there were serfs in Russia, and now . . .'

'Oh, Vasili, the Russians must work out their own destiny in their own way. But you don't really think that the Georgians, the Khazakhstanis, the Uzbeks, the Ukrainians and all the rest of them would stay in the Soviet Union for a day if they had the chance to be independent, do you?'

'But they are represented in the Praesidium.'

'Of course. By men who can be trusted to do what the Politburo wants.'

'But conditions are so much better now. There is food, houses, education, work for all. The Soviets have done all this.'

'Let's forget it, my love. Don't let's argue.'

He smiled. 'You had no answer, did you?'

'To what?'

'To what I said. The improvements since the Tsar.'

She shook her head, smiling. 'You're saying that things have improved in sixty years. Of course they have. They've improved everywhere in the world. But what have the Russians got? A shortage of everything, from pots and pans to milk and butter – but plenty of nuclear bombs.'

'We have to defend ourselves, Inge.'

'Rubbish.'

Then she saw the hurt look on his face. 'I was going to tell you some news tomorrow, but maybe I'll tell you now. You and I are going to have a baby.'

He looked so surprised, and then so pleased that their differences were swept away in an orgy of planning from names to baby clothes.

They never talked about politics again, but the fact that they didn't, that there were things that couldn't be discussed, made its own sharp point. There were sometimes items in news bulletins that were so obviously distorted that he would glance guiltily towards her, and occasionally she smiled back at him without comment. As time went by he was sometimes the one to smile first.

Karpov was on one of his routine visits but it was only on his last day in Berlin that he called Burinski to his temporary office. He pointed to a chair, a brown file cover in his hand.

'How's your Dutch, Burinski?'

'I don't speak Dutch, comrade Karpov.'

'Well, you'll get by with German. I'm sending you to Holland for a couple of days. Have you heard of a town called Arnhem?'

'No, comrade Colonel.'

'It's not far from the German frontier. I want you to attend a funeral.'

Burinski sat silently. There was nothing to say.

'You'll have to leave tonight. There's an Aeroflot flight to Warsaw at seven o'clock. You'll have fresh documents before you leave. You take the KLM flight to Amsterdam that gets you there just before midnight. You phone the home of our cultural attaché, Andreyev. He will send a car for you. It will be driven by a Dutch woman. You'll sleep at her apartment and she'll take you to Arnhem in the afternoon. She'll take you to a church. You'll attend the funeral of a Jugoslav named Djuranovic. You'll go on you own to the funeral. I want you to observe all that goes on. Particularly the people who are there. Afterwards the Dutch woman will pick you up outside the church and she will tell you of the arrangements for you to come back to Berlin. Any questions?'

'What do you want me to look for?'

'What I said. Everything. Watch what happens. Study the people. Particularly the principal ones. That's your brief.'

Karpov stood up to signal that the interview was over but when Burinski was at the door Karpov said, 'I hear your wife is pregnant, comrade. My congratulations. Maybe she should have it in Moscow to make sure that it's a genuine Soviet.'

Karpov was smiling, but his hard grey eyes were intent on Burinski's reactions.

'I think my wife wants to have the baby in Weimar to be near her parents.'

Karpov shrugged. 'Bear it in mind, comrade Burinski, bear it in mind. These things get noticed.'

And Karpov nodded his final dismissal.

The coffin was carried by six men from the hearse, through the arched gate to the churchyard. There were twelve people following the coffin. Only one of them was well-dressed, a man with a shaven head and a pale, impassive face. He glanced briefly at Burinski and then joined the others as they walked into the church.

It was a short service, without ceremony. A prayer, a hymn, an oration in a foreign language that Burinski guessed was Serbo-Croat, a final prayer, then what sounded like a national anthem as the coffin was carried down the aisle. It was a small church and a small graveyard long and narrow, with a gentle slope down a gravel path to a line of cypress trees.

A lean old man stood holding a shiny spade at the side of the freshly dug grave. He doffed his workman's cap as the coffin approached and stood back so that the mourners could gather round the graveside. There was only one woman. An elderly woman in black, with the tanned, leathery face of a gypsy. She held a small bunch of red and white carnations in her hand. Six or seven blooms.

The priest stood at the head of the open grave and as the coffin was lowered he intoned a prayer in Latin. The priest was a big, tall man, dark-skinned with bright blue eyes, and the light breeze lifted his thin hair as he bent down to throw a handful of soil into the grave. Four or five men nearest the grave did the same. The woman in black threw in the carnations and the priest signalled to the grave-digger to fill in the grave. The heap of clay soil was on the far side of the grave and as the first clods thudded on to the coffin the priest spoke again in the foreign tongue and this time it wasn't a prayer, it was a speech, an oration. The man spoke with passion as a plane flew overhead, the noise obliterating his words. And faces were lifted to the sky in irritation. As the noise abated, the priest finished his speech and the mourners followed him back to the church where they stood in small groups. And only the well-dressed man with the shaven head watched Burinski as he walked alone to the gate.

He walked along the country road towards the village and a few minutes later the Dutch woman pulled up the car alongside him.

His orders were to take a commercial flight from Schiphol, Amsterdam to Heathrow, London, where an embassy car and a colleague would be waiting for him.

It seemed a pointless journey. The car and the junior KGB man picked him up at Heathrow and drove him to the embassy. Burinski stayed there for three days. They escorted him on walks through Kensington Gardens, he saw Buckingham Palace and Karl Marx's grave in Highgate cemetery, but that was all. Sightseeing trips but not even a mention of the funeral in Arnhem. And then, with only two hours notice, the flight back to Prague and then on to East Berlin. Karpov was back in Moscow and nobody mentioned his trip. For a few weeks he was occupied in the usual office duties of a KGB administrative officer. Checking documents and signals traffic, and for a few days, interrogating a low-grade West German agent who had been picked up in Magdeburg.

Karpov phoned him from Moscow, not mentioning his journey to Holland but congratulating him on the interrogation. There was a special mission he was to carry out and after that he would be given more interrogations of German-speakers so that he could be in Berlin when the child was born. He recognised that he was being officially absolved from persuading Inge that their child should be born in the Soviet Union. There would be some reason behind it all, but he had no idea what it was.

The special assignment came earlier than he had expected. It was late one afternoon when the signal arrived from Moscow saying that he was to fly there the next day.

Karpov himself met him in at Sheremetyevo and he was surprised when they drove through Moscow and out to the *Kamera* compound outside the city. The *Kamera* was seldom used for actual briefings. He was shown to a small, narrow room in one of the wooden huts where he left his single case, and then he was escorted back to Karpov's office.

Karpov took him over to a trestle table along one wall of the office and one by one he turned over seven photographs so that they lay face upwards, as if he were a gambler turning up his cards.

'Have you ever seen any of those before? Look carefully.'

They were photographs of seven faces. Five men and two women. Burinski looked at each one carefully and then for a long time at two of them. Eventually he pointed at the two. The first and the sixth in the row.

'I think I've seen those two before.'

'Where?'

'At the funeral in Holland.'

'Go on.'

'The man has shaved his head. But I'm sure he was there. And I think this woman was there. But she's much older now. I'd say twenty years older.'

'So how do you know it's the same one?'

'Her eyes. They were very fiery eyes. She looks like a gypsy woman. I'd say she was sixty. Here she was younger but it's still the same eyes and she still looks like a gypsy.'

'Tell me about the man.'

'He was different from the others. Well-dressed. Tall, maybe one eighty-five or even a little more. Angry looking. Or maybe stern is the right word. It was almost as if he were the boss or the leader of the people who were there.'

Karpov moved across to his desk and pointed to a chair as he opened a drawer in his desk with his other hand. He took out a small thin phial and put it carefully on the desk in front of him.

'I want you to see this, Burinski.' He held it up towards Burinski. 'This phial is made of lead. It's practically solid lead. There are a few drops of liquid inside it. If the smallest drop touches your skin you'll die. It'll take quite a time. Whatever medical treatment they give you will make no difference, because they won't know what's the matter with you. Not even when you're dead and they do an autopsy.' He put the lead phial carefully back in his drawer and took out a piece of paper. It was a draughtsman's section through something, with dimensions, and arrows with numbers. He pushed it across the desk so that Burinski could see it closer. 'That's a section through the spike of an umbrella. A special umbrella that's been produced by *Kamera* staff. The bottom of the spike unscrews. You put the phial in here. Doesn't matter which end goes in first. When you touch the release button on the handle the hypodermic needle pierces the phial and extends about half a centimetre. A prick from that will be enough. Understood?'

Burinski nodded. 'Yes, comrade Major.' His voice was low and uncertain.

'They'll show you how to use it. They've got dummies for you to practise on, and when they say you're ready you'll go to London. Your target is the man you saw at the funeral. The well-dressed man with the shaven head. You'll be given assistance in contacting him, and I'll be talking to you again before you leave.'

'Who is the man, comrade Major?'

Karpov shook his head. 'An enemy of the State. You don't need to know more. It should take no more than ten days at the most. You'll be back in good time for your wife's confinement.'

'Yes, comrade Colonel.'

And when he was standing he saluted. They were both in uniform and you didn't have to salute in special establishments. But something compelled Burinski to salute just to relieve his own tension.

From where they were standing on Chiswick Common they could see both Woodstock Road and Bath Road. Some mornings Vojnovic came the longer way to the underground station at Turnham Green. The house where he lived was at the far end of Abinger Road. A pleasant Victorian semi-detached house with bay windows up and down and a small front garden that had been paved over. There was only a handful of cultivated gardens in the road. The more political refugees from Slav countries have neither the time nor the inclination for gardening. Putting Eastern Europe to rights is a full-time occupation.

It seemed strange to Burinski at first to see the shaven-headed man in these different surroundings. He heard Polish, Czech, Croat and Ukrainian spoken in these suburban London streets while they were carrying out the surveillance, but the speakers looked as English as the English themselves. Sometimes there was a small give-away. Men who still wore trilby hats, and women who wore chiffon scarves as they had once worn them in Buda or Warsaw.

Augustin Vojnovic worked at a small import-export company with offices over a printing press in Hammersmith. Every morning including Saturday he walked from Abinger Road to Turnham Green station and took the underground. It was only three stops to Hammersmith Broadway and a five-minute walk to the office.

The assignment had not been difficult: Vojnovic had already been under surveillance and his habits were regular. The only problem was which end of his journey to deal with him. There were advantages both ways. The crowds at the station in the morning gave excellent cover, but Burinski's instinct was for the other end of the journey, and on the open street rather than inside the station.

Panov, under orders from the Embassy, treated him as the expert and merely provided assistance where his English was insufficient or his lack of knowledge of England would make him noticed. Panov was also responsible for checking that they themselves were not under surveillance. He was a Tass man, an efficient journalist who worked out of the main offices in the Press Centre just off Fleet Street. He lived in Highgate and was well dug-in in the student fraternity and with the left-wing intellectuals. He was in no hurry to be posted away from London, particularly to Moscow. It was the first time he had positively assisted in a KGB operation and he wanted it to go smoothly. KGB commendations could help careers and provide extra privileges.

Then they saw Vojnovic, his old-fashioned raincoat over his arm, his black briefcase in his other hand. He walked briskly, a soldierly walk, head held high and eyes to the front. As he went in to the station they crossed the main road. They had already bought weekly season tickets and they followed Vojnovic up the crowded stairway on to the eastbound platform. They travelled in the same carriage and walked slowly a few yards behind him in the crowds at Hammersmith. As usual he stopped at the small newsagents and bought a single packet of Gauloise's before carrying on to his office.

When they were sitting in the small snackbar just off Hammersmith Broadway Panov said, 'We've only got another two days, comrade.'

'I'll do it today. This evening. That's the best time.'

'But I thought . . .'

'You'd better make the travel arrangements for me right now. I'll be finished here by six-thirty. I'll show you where I shall want the car. It'll be by the dance hall.'

They eventually took a train to Hampstead and a taxi to Panov's place just off Highgate High Street. Panov went out to use a public telephone to make the travel arrangements and order a car and driver.

Burinski sat alone, the umbrella on the table alongside him as he read a tattered copy of *Anna Karenina*. He had always meant to read it but had somehow never got round to it. It was better than he had expected. It was one of his father's favourites. That and *War and Peace*. From time to time he put the book down, reached out for the umbrella and, holding it carefully he looked again at the little grey button on the handle. There was a terrible temptation to touch it, to press it. A temptation that increased as the hours passed.

Panov was back by midday, with cold meat and salad for their meal. At three o'clock they walked to the crossroads at Southwood Lane. A grey Volkswagen was waiting for them.

All three of them sat silently in the Volkswagen at the back of the playing fields at Hammersmith moving on from time to time to avoid the traffic wardens. At five o'clock Burinski got out. A few moments later Panov followed him, his eyes on the umbrella. He guessed it was some sort of weapon but he had no idea how it was to be used.

Burinski wanted to be able to walk in the same direction as Vojnovic but there were no shop windows to cover his loitering. There was a big public building and he stood near the entrance checking his watch as if he were waiting for someone.

It was five-thirty exactly when Vojnovic came through the door that the offices shared with the jobbing printer. He paused on the pavement, glancing up at the sky, then turned to walk to the station. Five paces behind, Burinski pressed the button and felt the slight jolt of the mechanism working. Increasing his stride until he was just behind his victim, he touched the umbrella spike to the back of the man's leg. Vojnovic turned his head quickly, frowning, and Burinski walked on and past him.

There was a woman traffic warden leaning down at the Volkswagen window, talking to the driver. As Burinski got to the car, the warden said something as she turned to walk away. Burinski could tell that it was some form of admonishment but he had no idea what it meant.

Panov pushed forward the front seat so that Burinski could get in the car and seconds later the car moved off. There were three or four people looking down at the man on the pavement; another person, a man, was crouching down undoing Vojnovic's shirt at the neck, then they were past. They turned into Goldhawk Road, crossed King Street and took the Great West Road in the direction of Heathrow.

Panov waited with him at the terminal until the SAS flight to Stockholm was called. Only then did Burinski carry out the *Kamera*'s final instruction and grind the spike of the umbrella against the concrete floor before handing it to Panov. And later that night it was pushed into the junk and rubble in a demolition company's yellow skip outside a deserted site in Aldgate.

At Bromma a man from the Stockholm Embassy had passed him his air ticket to East Berlin on a flight that left just after midnight. There was only half an hour to wait.

Karpov himself was waiting for Burinski at Schönefeld and listened attentively as he reported on his mission. Interested enough to put a few questions to him, nodding a tentative approval from time to time.

Vojnovic was unconscious for five hours before he came to in the emergency ward at Hammersmith Hospital. He complained of stomach pains and was treated for acute gastritis. But by the third day the treatment was obviously failing and he was put in a room on his own. Apart from the severe stomach pains nothing seemed wrong. Although he was unsteady on his feet he was able to walk to the toilets unaided. On the fourth day he was lethargic and weak but there were no medical indications of any disease or infection.

It was the sixth day when the situation changed drastically. When the duty nurse turned back the sheets to wake him she took one look and then, covering him again, she reported to the ward sister who telephoned for the duty doctor.

Vojnovic's breathing was shallow but even. As the ward sister and the doctor looked at his body they saw that it was criss-crossed with dark brown stripes and there were black and blue swellings on his face as well as his body. A thick, yellow secretion oozed from his eyelids and ran down his cheeks, and small pinheads of blood had seeped through the pores down one side of his body.

The doctor reached out and gently touched his chest, his belly and the side of his neck. The skin was dry, shrunken, and burning hot.

He turned to the ward sister who looked shocked. 'He's been poisoned. Get our emergency service to locate Professor O'Connor. He should be at St Thomas's. Otherwise try his home and his practice in Wimpole Street. Tell them that it's very urgent.'

The ward sister came back a few minutes later and stood

beside him. 'Patsy's tracing him. Is there anything we can do for the man?'

'Not until I've spoken to O'Connor. Watch.'

He reached forward and touched Vojnovic's scalp where his hair had sprouted while he was in the hospital. The stubble came away from the dry scalp as if it were dust.

'I'd say that it's thallium poisoning. And that means we had better notify the police if it's confirmed.'

'Why?'

'Thallium's a very rare toxic metal. It couldn't have been ingested accidentally. I doubt if even any hospital lab in London has any.'

'Who would have it?'

He turned to look at her and said softly, 'One of the secret government labs. O'Connor will know.'

A young man came hurrying in. Professor O'Connor was on the phone.

O'Connor came over himself an hour later and examined their patient. He confirmed that it was almost certainly thallium poisoning, wrote out a programme of treatment and telephoned himself to one of the Assistant Commissioners at Scotland Yard. He was given another number to contact and the AC laid on a police escort for bringing the antidotes by plane and motor cycle from Cornwall.

The antidotes arrived by RAF fighter at Northolt, and the police brought them the rest of the way. They were being administered six hours after the diagnosis. According to O'Connor the prognosis was reasonable provided there were no other complications.

Long before the antidotes arrived a uniformed police guard had been mounted outside Vojnovic's room.

O'Connor telephoned the number he had been given by Scotland Yard. It was a Cambridge number and the man he spoke to, Sir Arthur French, was only mildly interested until he asked the victim's name. When O'Connor said it was a Slav name he was asked to go over his comments again.

When Peter Nicholson showed his SIS identity card to the doctor in charge he was refused access to Vojnovic's room.

The patient was unconscious and was not to be disturbed. Nicholson did not insist on access that night.

After three days it was obvious that Vojnovic was dying. O'Connor came across twice a day to go over the results of the various tests. Vojnovic's white corpuscles were being swiftly and fatally destroyed, his bones were decaying, his saliva glands atrophying and his blood turning to plasma. In the early hours of the fourth morning he died.

Chapter 6

SIR ARTHUR FRENCH stood in the shelter of the station canopy at Leicester Square underground and looked up at the sky. The rain was teeming down, but there was a good patch of blue way over towards St Paul's. It was the third week of April so you could still expect the traditional showers. As he stood there, waiting for the rain to abate he wondered what Meynell would have to say. Meynell had talked with O'Connor and was concerned that SIS should be aware of the implications. And Luther Meynell wasn't a panic merchant. Nevertheless, he *had* suggested that the meeting should not be held at any of the official places. He had also suggested that Nicholson from the Soviet desk, and perhaps Anders, should also attend.

The rain stopped, but French put up his umbrella to hide his face as he walked up Charing Cross Road. It was a reflex rather than a real precaution. There were probably fewer than a couple of dozen people outside the security services who could identify him as the current head of MI6, and most of those would be members of foreign Intelligence services. But he was a cautious man and that caution was the main reason for his appointment. Some said that he was a bit of an old maid, a nagger, but there had been enough slap-happy administration in the service for the Foreign Office to prefer to put the clock back to the good old days.

In fact, Sir Arthur French was no more cautious than his appointment called for. It was he who had offered the funding for Anders' club to ensure that a valuable talent was not completely lost to SIS. It was merely that before he made certain types of decisions he liked to hear the opinion of others whose judgement he valued. And if the operation concerned was in any way offbeat he wanted somebody to check that it wasn't straying beyond its brief. Those who appointed him were well satisfied. Those who worked with him sometimes wondered what sort of man he really was.

On the steps of the club he shook the rain from his umbrella before turning to go inside. His eyes took in the general tattiness, and then Anders came up the stairs.

'Good afternoon, sir. Your other guests haven't arrived yet, would you rather wait here until they come, or go through to my place?'

'I think perhaps your place. Can somebody wait for them?'

'Of course.'

Anders used the internal phone and told Jacky to come up and wait for the two other guests. As Sir Arthur followed Anders down the stairs he said, 'You don't feel a coat of paint might improve the appearance in the . . . er . . . foyer?'

Anders laughed. 'It would, sir, but the customers would hate it. They never really notice what the place is like. The lights are low anyway, and they like everything to stay the same. They're a bit like children.'

'Do you get police in here, checking?'

Anders hesitated. Sorting out acceptable truth from shocking truth. Half a dozen policemen of various ranks were unofficial members of the club. There was an understanding that they were totally off duty and his more traditional members could ignore them, like herds of gazelle grazing contentedly under the gaze of lions who had already killed.

'They pop in from time to time. They're no problem.'

Anders unlocked both locks on the door to his suite and went in with Sir Arthur who accepted a Vichy water and looked at the spines of the books on the shelves.

'You've got a very catholic taste in books, Mr Anders. Are you a reader or a collector?'

Before Anders could reply there was a knock on the door. It was Peter Nicholson and Luther Meynell.

'Hello Tad. Are we first?'

'No. Come in. I'll leave you to it. You know where the

drinks are. Help yourselves and use the red phone if you want anything. Ask for me.'

'Right. Thanks.'

Luther Meynell poured himself a double whisky and Nicholson took a sherry.

Luther Meynell had a strong face, but his deep-set eyes and his downward curving mouth gave it a touch of grimness that was deceptive. He was a serious man but not grim. Not too far back there had been a Jewish grandma, a strong-willed woman who had moved her family from Berlin to Bermondsey and had prospered in the fur trade in London's East End. Born in 1930 into a middle-class family in Hampstead, Luther Meynell had the same determination. It was addressed not to commerce but to learning, and eventually to teaching. Even at Cambridge he wasn't sure whether his final interest would be languages or science.

His natural aptitude for languages he took for granted, and after graduating he had done his National Service in the Intelligence Corps. Commissioned almost immediately, he had been a captain by the time his service was over. Against his expectations he had enjoyed his time in the Army. His fellow officers were intelligent, with lively minds, and when he had been offered a permanent post in the Foreign Office he had taken only twenty-fours to think about it before he accepted. The urge to the academic life was still there, but the job in MI6 appealed to him.

He had that rare ability to reduce complex problems to their simplest equation, and exercising that talent on significant problems appealed to him. Although his talent had been much in demand it had not led to startling advancement. In SIS in the late fifties and early sixties, internal politics and personal relationships had too often controlled promotion. When, in 1972 he had been offered a chair at his old college he hadn't hesitated. He had taken early retirement and a reduced pension, and with the unanimous good wishes of his colleagues he had gone off to teach.

By then he had a family. Two girls. His choice of a wife had surprised his friends. She was younger than he, a strikingly pretty short-story writer of considerable talent. Perhaps his young wife was the only person who knew that behind that rather immobile face and incisive mind there was a sensitivity that he deliberately kept hidden. It was a sensitivity that made him reach for solutions in deeds rather than words. You didn't console the drowning. You fished them out.

When he had made himself comfortable Meynell turned to look at French. 'I arranged with Professor O'Connor to attend the autopsy. It was done at St Thomas's because they had facilities he needed.' He paused. 'It took over a week, Arthur. It was very meticulously done. And I'm afraid there's no doubt that it was murder. And, I suppose, more assassination than murder.'

'How can you be sure of that?'

'Only a government laboratory could have supplied either the know-how or the material. According to O'Connor we couldn't have done it ourselves. We could now. But you'd have to have scientists specifically briefed to find a means of killing a man without leaving any evidence. And they would need to have access to all available written information to come up with this particular solution. Even then I would estimate that it must have taken them at least two years to achieve this . . . this terrible success. It's complex, expensive, almost fool-proof, and incredibly vicious.'

'Tell us more, Luther.'

Meynell hesitated for a moment. It wasn't easy to describe to non-scientists. Whatever you said it would be slightly inaccurate.

'Well let's start with thallium. From the Greek *thallos* – a green shoot. Shoot like plants have. Called thallium because it has a brilliant green stripe in its spectrum. It's a rare metal, found in very small quantities in iron and copper pyrites. It's bluish-white in colour and looks a bit like lead. It has one other property. It's highly toxic. However, there are antidotes against thallium poisoning. We used them all to treat this man but we were on a wild goose chase. We were doing exactly what we were meant to do. We were wasting vital hours. I'm not sure that we could have done anything even if we had known what the real problem was.'

'What was the real problem?'

'The thallium had been subjected to intense atomic radiation which causes the metal to disintegrate into tiny particles. We still don't know how it was introduced into the man's body, and I suspect we never will, but as soon as it was in him, perhaps by food or drink, the radio-active particles disintegrated completely and permeated his system with deadly radiation.' Meynell paused. 'Who was he, Arthur?'

'A Jugoslav. He had worked for the KGB and then changed his mind. He defected about three years ago with his family. He wasn't a normal defector because he was still a convinced Communist. But he'd changed his mind about Moscow and decided that Tito was right to be independent. Obviously Tito's people were suspicious and he wasn't sure what their reaction would be if he went back. We let him stay here. He filled in a few holes for us. More confirmation than revelation, and he was building his bridges back to Jugoslavia. He headed a group of Serbo-Croats in Europe who were pro-Tito. They weren't all that effective but I suspect they raised the blood-pressure a bit in Moscow.'

'So Moscow have him murdered to discourage others.'

'It seems like it.'

Nicholson shifted in his chair but said nothing. Not so much from diffidence but because he was conscious of his youth compared with the other two.

'Can we prove this, Luther?'

'It depends what you mean by prove. We have enough factual information recorded to convince any competent forensic scientist. But if you mean the public then forget it. Start using words like thallium and they'll turn the page. And they're used to stories about dirty tricks by the KGB. Even if they believe them it doesn't surprise them.'

'But sending someone to London to assassinate a man just to *décourager les autres* is outrageous by any standards.'

'Is it? Even after the Arabs?'

'For us it's very different from the Arabs. The KGB are professionals. They know we won't knuckle under on this sort of issue. They see the Arabs as fanatics. Lunatics. And they're not far wrong. But to me this is a very dangerous precedent.'

'Of course. But you're a professional. You know the rules and you know these chaps are breaking the rules. But all that is meaningless to the public.'

Nicholson turned to look at his boss. 'If we let them get away with this, God knows where it will stop. They can start putting *us* on the list. It's not difficult for them here but our chances of retaliating in Moscow are almost nil.'

French raised his eyebrows. 'So what do you suggest?'

'I don't know. I'd need to think about it. But right now my mind goes to the guy downstairs.'

'You mean Anders?'

'Yes.'

'What do you think, Luther?'

'Maybe Peter's right. But I suggest we all think about it for a couple of days.' He turned to look at French. 'Are you going to be up at the cottage at the weekend?'

'I expect so.'

'Perhaps we could meet then.'

'OK. I'll call you tomorrow to fix a time.'

Peter Nicholson stayed behind after the other two had left. Anders and he were more of an age, and although they were very different kinds of men they got on well together.

Peter Nicholson was thirty-eight, with an actor's handsome face. He had toyed with the idea of an acting career in his last year at Winchester and during his time at Oxford. He was almost too handsome not to be an actor. It was a Roman emperor's face with large features. Men noticed his eyes but women noticed the full sensuous mouth. A tendency towards corduroy suits only emphasised the theatricality of his face. When he walked in the street young women openly stared and, recovering their composure, discovered that they were lost and turned to the handsome man for help in directing them on their way. And in restaurants homosexual waiters clamoured to serve him. Although he was aware of his good looks he was genuinely indifferent to the heads that turned, and the overt flattery.

His father was a High Court judge. Handsome, but not so extravagantly handsome as his eldest son, his face looked saturnine under his judge's wig. And guilt-ridden prisoners in the dock saw menace in the thick black eyebrows and piercing eyes. The less guilty were more aware of the judge's total absorption in what was being said. With two sons and three daughters Mr Justice Nicholson lived a full, rather Victorian life between the small flat in Chelsea and the sprawling manor house in Sussex. It was a civilised life with a wide circle of interesting friends and acquaintances, the only criterion he and his wife applied when issuing a second invitation was that their guest should have an enquiring, lively mind. A family friend had likened it all to a modern version of the Bloomsbury set.

Peter Nicholson had taken Winchester and Oriel College in his stride, seemingly immune to the barbarities of English public schools, and capable of enjoying both the academic and social life at Oxford. He came from a privileged family and it gave him a kind of invisible armour against the world. His wife came from a similar background of privilege, wealth and the arts. Beautiful, French and chic she brought a sharp dressing to his rather mellow life. He had been recruited into SIS during his last year at Oxford and his promotions had been slow as they weighed him up. He had met his wife Fleur during his two years in Paris but when he was posted to Moscow it was almost another three years before they met again. Two months later they were married in the church at Perigueux and after a short honeymoon he had gone back to Oriel for an advanced Russian course. Nicholson had been Deputy Head of the Russian desk at SIS for nearly three years.

Nicholson poured himself another sherry.

'I saw your Judy last week.'

'Which judy was that?'

Nicholson laughed. 'You cheeky bastard. The one *called* Judy.'

'Oh. Where was she?'

'A dinner party. At the Fawcetts'. She was there with her husband but neither of them looked too happy about it. Has she gone back to him?'

'Not that I know of.' Anders sighed. 'How did she look?'

'And oh what ails thee knight at arms, alone and palely loitering et cetera, et cetera. She looked attractive, a bit drawn, rather haunted eyes, and she was trying very hard to be the life and soul of the party. Or maybe just the centre of attention.' He looked at Anders' face. 'I'd say she was high as a kite and that it wasn't just on grass.'

'And her husband?'

'Much as usual. Po-faced. Pompous. The successful barrister. Holding his breath in case his wife was so far gone that she started using four-letter words to show how with-it she is.'

'Did she?'

'No. She flaked out about ten-thirty. Everybody was very understanding.' Nicholson sighed. 'Why the hell do you waste you time with a bunch like that?'

'Only one of them.'

'Oh, Tad. Don't play God or the knight in shining armour. She's one of them, tough as steel, eye on the main chance and utterly selfish. There's hundreds of 'em around. They're poison, Tad.'

'She needs help.'

'Sure she does. But not your kind of help. She needs a psychiatrist or a kick up the backside. Why get mixed up with them, Tad? Her whole family are a bunch of creeps and I'll bet she gave that husband of hers a rough ride.'

'He seems to be coming back for more.'

'He's a Catholic. He's got to, but I bet he isn't enjoying it.'

'D'you want to go downstairs for a bit?'

'If he'll play my tunes.' Nicholson grinned.

'What tunes?'

' "Manhattan" for me and "La Mer" for my old lady.'

'How is she?'

'Everybody's fine.' He put his hand on Anders' shoulder. 'I wish I could get you fixed up nice and cosy.'

Sir Arthur French went back to his flat in Albany and boiled an egg, made some toast and poured coffee from the Cona. When he had finished eating he cleared away, washed up and walked back into the sitting room.

It was too late to ring Mrs Griggs, his housekeeper at the cottage. He reached out for the copy of Verlaine's *Romances sans Paroles* and walked slowly to his bedroom. The cottage was just outside Cambridge on the Trumpington Road, and once upon a time he'd been happy there. Sometimes he envied Verlaine, who had had the courage to shoot at his rival. Only a wound in the wrist and it hadn't done any good. But it had improved his poetry. He wondered what it was that had made Vera despise him. It had been a difficult time, and he had tried very hard. To no avail. There had been a series of men before she went off with the shifty solicitor from Bury St Edmunds. Sir Arthur had been glad when it was all over. It had caused him pain but not grief, and it had taught him a lesson. He now shared Somerset Maugham's jaundiced view of women, and valued his freedom more than that short year of happiness.

Chapter 7

LUTHER MEYNELL stood with his hands in his pockets looking out of the window of French's small study next to his bedroom. A dark female thrush stood on the lawn just below the window. Her thin legs braced, her head to one side, then savagely attacking the lawn, tugging at a fat, wet worm. Creatures ordered their lives so much better than men, he thought. The decades, even the centuries, had made no difference to them. A seventeenth-century thrush would have led a life no different from the one on the lawn. But seventeenth-century man, and now twentieth-century man . . . He turned impatiently away from the window. His thoughts were being diverted.

He walked back to the table, touched the brown folder, then reached for the cup and slowly sipped what was left of the cold coffee. He walked out to the small landing, the cup still in his hand.

'Arthur? Are you there Arthur?'

'Coming.'

Sir Arthur French was wearing a pair of plastic gloves and a flowered pinafore, and Luther Meynell wondered what would happen to a Director of the KGB who appeared in such a garb. It was both endearing and rather frightening, and, he thought, very typically British.

'Let's sit down and talk, Arthur.'

They sat facing each other across the small mahogany table, the file pushed to one side.

'Your people have done a first-class job with so little to go on. The first two proposals are right out, to my mind. They're just revenge operations. And Moscow may not even recognise them as such. We don't learn anything and we may not make our point. But the third scheme is a possible. The one using

Anders. The right experience and the right temperament. A lot of useful information for us and a real lesson for them, not only for the top boys but for any other operatives they might be thinking of using in the future. But the suggestion of a public trial isn't on. The media would have a field-day. The public would love it, of course: British agent goes into enemy territory and brings back assassin to justice. That would last a couple of days and then you'd have a pompous leader in *The Times* – can we complain about Arab kidnappings – encouraging retaliation – murder in the streets of London. You could end up with a vote of censure in the UN if they played their cards well.'

'What about Anders himself?'

'Ideal. It's lucky you kept him on.'

'Your suggestion, my friend.'

Meynell shrugged. 'He'll need some back-up.'

'I can't let many people in on it. It's got to be off the record. Private enterprise on Anders' part. No official knowledge of what was going on. And if he makes a cock-up it's all his. I don't want to know.'

Meynell smiled and shrugged. 'He must be used to that by now, Arthur. Official hypocrisy.'

'There's no other way, Luther.'

'Of course not. It's just that the Russians do it better.'

'Yes. I suppose they do. The blessings of dictatorships. How about a sherry before you go?'

'No thanks. We've got guests this evening – why don't you join us? It's informal. Only a handful.'

'No. Odd men are always a damn nuisance. Thanks all the same.'

'Don't be ridiculous, it's just a cold spread and a debate about whether small really is beautiful. You'd enjoy it.'

He saw French hesitate and chipped in. 'We'll expect you at eight. Pullover and slacks. OK?'

'I'll look forward to it.'

As Luther Meynell cycled back the two miles to his own home he felt sad for the lonely man who had once been his chief. He hoped that he was better at choosing undercover men than he was at choosing wives. A schoolboy would have seen that the beautiful Vera was vain to the point of mania, and would need her ego polished by a dozen men to hold her neuroses in check. But intelligent men seemed as prone as fools to wrong judgements about pretty women. When he chose his pretty Patsy it hadn't been because he *needed* someone but because he *wanted* her, and that was a very different thing. It would be a good discussion point at a Saturday night get-together. Need is negative, want is positive. Discuss.

Anders recognised Peter Nicholson's voice immediately.

'Can I come over and see you, Tad?'

'Sure. When?'

'You tell me.'

'Right now if you want. We don't open for another couple of hours.'

'OK. I'll come right over.'

'Is it business or pleasure?'

He heard Nicholson's soft laugh. 'You crazy loon. Can you imagine me coming to that dump for pleasure?'

Anders smiled as he hung up. It was nearly an hour before Nicholson arrived. Anders noticed that he was carrying a brief-case. They walked along the corridor and up to his rooms.

'D'you want a drink, Peter?'

'After we've talked, if I get a second chance.'

Nicholson took out a pale green file cover and a large brown envelope and placed them on the coffee table.

'It's a briefing, Tad.'

'Where?'

'We're not sure but it looks like Berlin. East Berlin.'

'Is this the Jugoslav murder thing?'

'Yes. What have you heard?'

'Nothing. I just read the very brief reports in the papers. They seemed a bit guarded and low-key so I assumed that it was KGB. What happened?'

Nicholson tipped up the brown envelope and a dozen or so photographs slid out. Some black and white, and some

Polaroid colour prints. He took out two or three of the colour prints.

'A bit grainy and the colours not absolutely accurate but enough for you to see what happened.'

Nicholson sat silently as Anders looked slowly and carefully at the photographs, until without looking up he said, 'How did they do it?'

He listened intently as Nicholson explained what they had been told. When he finished Anders looked up at his face.

'And you want me to knock him off?'

'No. We want you to bring him back.'

'Who is he?'

'We're pretty sure he's a guy named Burinski. A traffic warden saw a man get into a Volkswagen just after the Jugoslav went down. It was parked on a double-yellow line and she'd taken its number but the driver was a foreigner and she'd let him go after the passenger got in. We traced the car. It was hired but we did a bit of ferreting and discovered that it had been hired by a Russian named Panov. He works as a journalist at the Tass set-up.

'He was obviously scared and we put the frighteners on him and then dangled a few carrots. He likes it in the West and we let him phone his office and say he'd got the flu. We've got someone with him at his rooms.

'He's given us all he knows about this guy Burinski. It seems Burinski is KGB. Vasili Burinski. Early thirties. Married with one kid. Son of a retired Red Army General and it looks like he's an operator with the *Spetsburo*. Lives in East Berlin and based at the MfV HQ in Normannenstrasse. We've got an artist's impression of him that Panov swears is a good likeness. That's about all we've got at the moment.'

'How the hell do I get him out, for God's sake? Why do I have to bring him back?'

'We want to find out a number of things, Tad. Was this a one-off emergency job? Are they planning more? Are they testing out our reaction? There's a lot we want to know. There's no obvious reason why it should be an emergency. The Jugoslav wasn't that important. There's hundreds like him all over the world. Not ex-KGB maybe, but dissidents organising other dissidents. They aren't a real danger to the Soviet Union, not even in their twisted minds.'

'Maybe they struck at that level so that we wouldn't react too strongly.'

'Could be. But whatever the reason was, our masters have decided that he's going to be lifted and brought back here.'

'What back-up do I get?'

'As little as possible. I'll give you all the technical help you need and I'll get as much background as I can. But when you're there it'll be you on your own. It's absolutely unofficial. We know nothing about it. We've never heard of you. It's all just a KGB frame-up.' He paused. 'I'm sorry, Tad. But you know how it is. Even if you were still in the old firm it would be much the same. We couldn't acknowledge you or lift a finger. The KGB would know we were bluffing, just the same as they do, but with you it has to be for real. We really would have to abandon you if anything went wrong.'

'Who will be my contact in Berlin?'

'Andy Pritchett.'

'Jesus. That's a good start. Why him?'

'Because he's there. I know you don't like him, but he's tough and efficient and he knows his way around Berlin.'

'Has he been told?'

'Not yet.'

'Why don't you use him instead of me?'

Nicholson half-smiled. 'You're fishing for compliments. He doesn't speak Russian and . . .' he shrugged, '. . . he's just not the right man for the job. You are.'

'Let me think about it, Peter. I'm not sure I want it.'

'Why not?'

'There's too much to go wrong. Especially on a freelance basis. When I've got him over the frontier or through the Wall I've still got the West Germans to contend with. I'm going to need a hell of a lot of documentation for the other side of the Wall. Passport, travel documents, visas. Different nationalities and different names. And a lot of money. Dollars, krugerrands, sovereigns, the lot.'

'That's no problem, Tad. I don't understand why you're so . . . cautious – or whatever it is.'

'I'm cautious, friend, because of what's happened in the past. I cleared up an operation completely but because I went over the top for personal reasons I was thrown out. No talking, no discussion, no beating round the bush. I came to from the drugs and the second they were sure I could hear, they told me the good news. I was dangerous, they said, but I had my uses. All was not lost. So here I am, in my tatty little club where you all hold your skirts aside so that they don't catch the germs. But it's my leather couch that guys lie on while I fish a slug out of a shoulder or a leg. My bed that men sleep in when it's all got too much. And it's me you turn to when you need things doing that are just a bit too slimy for the good boys to touch.'

Nicholson looked at Anders for a long time before he spoke.

'That was all a long time ago, Tad. I hadn't realised that it still irked you. That was stupid of me. Stupid of all of us. Nobody wanted to do it. And it was Mac who told you because he was your friend. It must have seemed terribly unfair to you. You obviously *still* feel it was unfair. There wasn't any other way. Both SIS and 5 were in total disfavour with the politicians. The frogman thing with Crabb at Portsmouth still hung over us like a big black warning. When Macmillan moved Dick White from head of 5 to head of SIS it was a punishment as well as a warning.' He sighed, 'I'm sorry, Tad. I really am.'

'We'd better meet again tomorrow. What time?'

'I'll come about ten if that'll suit you.'

'OK.'

Anders walked with him to the street door but he didn't answer when Nicholson said, 'Ciao'.

In the taxi Nicholson sat with his head back against the top of the seat. He had seen tears round the edges of Tad Anders' eyes. And Anders wasn't the kind of man for tears. He would talk to Luther and Arthur French about it. Anders was big and tough, and a born loner, but they'd obviously taken him too much for granted. Everybody assumed that it was all water under the bridge. A single dud event that had had to happen. Long forgotten. But they were wrong. They had all taken it for granted that time would heal the wound for Tad Anders. But it hadn't. It sounded like time had made it worse. He must loathe them all. Taking him for granted. Happily using him to do their dirty work. Condescending to him in that tatty club. The old family retainer put out to graze, to be visited for a cup of tea when you happened to be in the vicinity. God, how stupid they'd been.

Anders was shaving when the internal phone rang. He looked at his watch on the hook at the edge of the mirror. It was 7.45, a quarter of an hour before they officially opened. As he lifted the phone Jacky said, 'Miss Judy's here to see you, Mr Anders.'

'Bring her up, Jacky. You can leave the desk.'

'Right, sir.'

Anders still used a blade and soap and he stood waiting for her with his face half smooth half lather. She was smiling and she looked pretty, and she smelled of Madame Rochas as she put up her mouth to be kissed. She stood looking up at his face, her arms round his neck, her body close to his.

'Why haven't you phoned me, Charles?'

'You said not to, sweetie.'

'Did I? How stupid. Maybe you misunderstood.'

'Maybe. Anyway, nice to see you. D'you want a sherry?'

'You finish shaving and I'll help myself.'

'OK. You do that. The evening paper's on the settee.'

When he had shaved and put on his tie and jacket he joined her on the settee. But he noticed that it wasn't sherry she was drinking. It was a large neat whisky and the bottle was on the table, alongside her glass.

'What have you been doing?'

She screwed up her nose, thinking. 'Nothing much. I've been trying to get a job.'

'What kind of job?'

'Oh, modelling, anything a bit glam would do.'

'I heard you were back with your husband.'
'Who told you that?'
'Does it matter?'
She shrugged irritably. 'I'm not, actually. I just met him a few times to talk, that's all.'
'How did you get on?'
'As usual. Bloody awful.'
'What happened?'
'He told me the conditions if I wanted to go back.'
'What were they?'
'I go to confession every week. I learn how to cook. I keep proper household accounts to be examined weekly. I get no cash dress allowance, just credit at two stores. No cheque book. No trips on my own. A regular medical check for alcohol and drugs and I adopt what he calls "a proper supportive role as his wife".'
'What did you think of all that?'
'I told him to get stuffed. What do you think of it?'
Anders smiled. 'It sounds like Monty's surrender document to the Germans.'
'D'you want to make love to me, Tad?'
'Why don't you stay the night?'
'I can't.'
'Why not?'
'He's having me watched. He'd got a whole sheaf of reports from a detective agency. He read me out a letter from his solicitor that said if I was out with a man after midnight the court would look on it in an unfavourable light. Why on earth should a barrister need a solicitor to tell him what the law is?'
'It's called getting things on the record. And reading it out is just to scare you.'
'It depresses me.'
'Why?'
'All of it depresses me. I feel lonely. An outcast. And I haven't really done much to deserve it.'
He took her hand and walked with her to his bedroom. As he undressed she pulled up her skirt and opened her legs as he lay alongside her.

'D'you like touching me there, Tad?'
'You know I do.'
'Do it to me, Tad. Do it to me now. Quickly.'
And when it was over she said softly, 'Was I good?'
'You were wonderful honey.'
'How about you get me another drink?'
As he sat on the edge of the bed and watched her drink the whisky he was sorry for her. He knew exactly how she felt.
'I'd better go, Tad.'
'Come down in the club and let Baldy play you a couple of tunes.'
She shook her head. 'I don't like it down there.'
'You'll be with me.'
She looked up at his face. 'Tad?'
'What is it?'
'I'm broke, Tad, will you lend me some money?'
He felt suddenly cold but he said, 'Of course I will. How much do you need?'
'Is a hundred too much?'
'No. Is it enough?'
'Yes.'
He walked with her to Charing Cross Road and waited until he was able to wave down a taxi for her. She got in and gave an address in Belgrave Square and only as the taxi pulled away did she remember and turn to wave to him. Her eyes looked as if she were already somewhere far away.

They talked for four hours and the table was covered with maps and papers that overflowed onto the floor.
'What do you feel about it, Tad?'
'Frankly it stinks. But if you're desperate then I'll do it, but it ought to be done properly. A full back-up team, a radio net, safe-house in East Berlin, route back properly planned and support people on the other side of the wall. There's no proper surveillance, all I can do is go straight in and out. And God knows how I get an unwilling man through the check point.'

'Let's go and have some lunch and talk about it again this afternoon.'

'OK. But why the hurry on this job?'

'He might get posted back to Moscow or somewhere that's even less accessible than Berlin.'

'Any chance of surveillance before I go in?'

'It's possible. Let's go and eat.'

They walked through Soho and ate at Leoni's, and by the time they were back at Anders' place he had thawed out enough for Nicholson to get down to positive planning.

'Let's go over the minimum you need, Tad, to give it a better than fifty-fifty chance.'

'I need someone over the other side. Preferably with accommodation and access to a vehicle. I need a radio net back to Pritchett and I need the documentation we've discussed. And I need the money already over there so that I don't have to take it in myself.'

'Why do you need a vehicle? You'd never get it through the check point with a body in it. Not even if you drugged him.'

'I won't be coming through the check point.'

'Tell me more.'

'Any check point is out unless you've got a full operation.'

'So where?'

'I want to use the place we've got in the Harz mountains.'

'I'll have to apply, Tad. And they're terribly uptight about using that.'

'It's that or a blind attempt up on the Baltic coast. There's no other way.'

'Let me check on it. I'll see what I can do. The other things you mentioned should be OK. We've had difficulty getting cash through recently but I think we can do it. How much do you need?'

'At least five thousand. Pounds not dollars. Eight would be better.'

'If I can fix those things how soon can you go?'

'Four hours' notice will be enough.'

Chapter 8

ANDERS SAT with his canvas bag between his feet. The Lufthansa girl had offered to put it up on the rack for him but he'd told her it was all the luggage he had and she let him bend the rules. She was obviously aware that he had been escorted by Airport security to the aircraft. It was Friday night and Gatwick was beginning its heavy weekend holiday traffic. There were eight planes ahead of them, waiting to take their turn on the main runway. It had been raining for most of the afternoon but the sky was cloudless now, a pale blue, and the watery sun cast long shadows from the equipment around the loading-bay.

It was nearly forty minutes before the under-carriage thudded into its housing and there were lights in the tiny model houses on the ground. Almost without thinking, Anders slid his right hand inside his jacket to check that the pistol was in place. He squeezed the base of the soft leather holster and felt the butt rise up under his arm and his thumb stretched out to touch lightly the grid on the safety-catch. Sir Arthur himself had got him clearance at both ends.

The plane was half empty. Berlin had its tourists, but not enough from London to fill a plane on a Friday evening, and the two seats beside him were both empty.

Nicholson had worked hard to get him everything he had asked for. There was only five thousand but it was mainly gold coin and the rest was dollars. It would be available night or day from the bookshop in Unter den Linden. The password was '*Abschied*' and the response was '*Servus*'. The contact man was Willi Kraus and there was a bed for him at the garage workshop. Anders had worked with Willi two or three times before. He was stolid and efficient and there would be no problems there. Luther Meynell had phoned him that morning and wished him luck in his guarded professorial way. And Nicholson had brought a message from French to say that Stoppard would keep an eye on the club for him until he was back. They had allowed seven days from start to finish, not counting the evening flight.

He had phoned Judy two days running but there had been no reply. Candy had stayed with him the last two nights. He had told her he was going to visit his father's family in Poland. She had asked him about them. What they did, and the details of their families, and he had felt ashamed when she bought two dolls for his nieces. There was something wrong with his life since Marie-Claire. Up to then his life had seemed always to be under control.

He had been successful as an SIS officer. Not spectacularly successful, but he had done what was asked of him and had been part of a team. His private life had been uneventful. Girlfriends, but with neither party too intense or dependent.

Marie-Claire had changed all that. It was as if she had opened some magic door from his ordinary world and taken him into a garden. But that tombstone in the church at Marlow had marked the end of all that. Sometimes he thought that in fact it had ended his life. Nothing had really gone right since then. It was like the seven lean years in the Bible. Which meant that there was still another year to go. His routine, controlled life in SIS had gone overnight. He was now what they officially referred to as a 'special-category operator'. No longer part of a team, no longer a member of that special club whose members know what is really going on in the world. Almost no longer British. Just a Polish hoodlum who spoke good English. Like Kipling's description – 'the lesser breeds without the law'. Without consciously intending it, Anders had wrapped the tatty club around him like a protective cloak. It was his only home, and over the years he had come to have more in common with the criminal extroverts he mixed with every night than with his former colleagues. They passed no moral judgements and if he had asked it of them they would have arranged, without any question, the elimination of anyone who threatened his peace of mind. But if they never saw him again he would be forgotten in a couple of months. He didn't belong with them. They tolerated him amiably, as SIS tolerated him. He lived from day to day. He no longer had ambitions or even expectations. He had somehow lost the art of living, he just existed. He had money and he had his health, and most of the time that was enough. But there were times when he had to escape. And the cottage outside Battle was his retreat. He had told nobody about it and he was sure that even SIS were not aware of its existence. But in two or three days of peace and sleep he could charge the batteries of his mind to face going back to his grey, grim world.

The cottage was isolated but he was never lonely there. His books and his music were all that he needed. And his thoughts. In that private limbo his life had a future. He had no idea what it was, but as more normal mortals have their vague dream of heaven, he had vague dreams of a better future, and tried to find the patience to await its arrival. No doubt the people who knew him in his other life would have found it incredible. That was because they looked without seeing. But in a way it was no more strange to dream of merely being happy than to dream of being a painter in Tahiti, the owner of a pub in Devon, or winning the Pools.

Anders was asleep by the time they passed over the ragged coastline of Holland. Ten minutes out from Tegel and the captain's announcement that they were on time for landing had woken him. Like most SIS field agents he was used to snatching sleep when he could, and he could come out of even the deepest sleep to instant awareness. He moved his right foot to check that the bag was still there, slid his hand inside his jacket and went through the reflex routine of checking his pistol, and then leaned back, relaxed in his seat. He wished that it wasn't to be Pritchett as his back-up in Berlin. He wasn't sure why he didn't like the man. He was competent and amiable, but there was a cockiness there that bordered on arrogance. Self-confidence was a plus in their game, but over-confidence could be fatal. But he wouldn't be all that dependent on Pritchett.

Andy Pritchett was sitting on a red stool in the airport bar, sipping a malt whisky and gazing at the sweater of a young blonde on the other side of the circular bar. She'd got a bedroom look in her big blue eyes but he guessed she was just practising. She wasn't more than eighteen.

Andrew Pritchett had never lacked for either girlfriends or bedfellows and they weren't always synonymous. In his middle thirties, with only a wisp of blonde hair between him and baldness he had one of those worn, bag-eyed faces that had suddenly come into fashion with the new men in Hollywood. Not plain, and certainly not ugly, but the deep lines from nose to mouth and the aggressive piercing grey eyes gave him an openly macho image that, despite women's lib, girls and women still seemed to find attractive.

He didn't fancy this operation with Anders. Unless they'd been holding out on him it didn't seem well enough prepared. Not enough background and not enough planning. Gung-ho operations worked in wartime, but in Berlin now the pieces were all laid out very carefully on the chess board, and the rules of the game were precise. There was no room for amateurs when you were playing games with the KGB. And what made it worse was that Anders didn't like him. He wasn't sure why, but others had said that it was resentment: that they both operated in the same violent area of SIS but Anders had been pushed outside while he was still on the establishment. It probably *had* been unfair but if you put up a black like Anders had done you could expect to get your head chopped off. And they hadn't done that. They'd just shuffled him to one side. His own life and career had been even more unorthodox than Anders' but he had kept just inside the rules. And that didn't include literally slicing up a man's belly and pulling his guts out. Especially when the man was already dead or dying. Maybe it was like people had said. Once a Slav always a Slav, and despite Anders' upbringing and his mother's genes it was the Slav bit that came out in crises. The Slav bit was pretty useful. But not in a civil servant. And cut the cake whichever way you fancied, SIS was part of the Foreign Office and they *were* all civil servants. Index-linked pensions and all.

Pritchett ordered another double whisky and sat there sipping it slowly and thinking. His whole life seemed to have been a progress through the criminal calendar. Thrown out of Eton for putting the girl from the sweetshop in the family way. Four years crewing on luxury yachts, the last two running guns from Marseilles to Crete, Tunisia, Turkey and Libya. A year as chucker-out at a St Tropez night-club and more girl trouble. Knife trouble. His knife. Then the job as a salesman of Rolls-Royces and Bentleys in Rome, when, after a few months, he'd been invited by the owner to meet a friend in a café on the Via Veneto. And a week later he was being interviewed in a private room at the Connaught. An interview that saw him recruited into SIS. Or, to be more exact, recruited to an unestablished post in the Foreign Office. He was always amazed that people saw him as prone to violence and as having an exaggerated independence of authority.

His father was delighted that his son was what he referred to as a member of the Foreign Office, and he did nothing to disturb the old man's peace of mind. As vicar of a small village in the West Country his father was the kindest man he had ever known. Nothing that he had ever done had forfeited the old man's love. Married in middle-age to a charming younger woman, he was an elderly father, but when Andy Pritchett's mother had died in a sanatorium when he was ten, the Reverend Anthony Pritchett had become father and mother to the young boy. He was probably neither a very good father nor a competent mother, but every minute of his life was devoted to the boy. There was almost no discipline, and his father had never read Spock. But they walked for miles through the countryside and the old man knew every wildflower and animal and how they lived. And in the evenings they read together. Not the books he had at the village school, but anything from Thomas Hardy to Plato. He was always amazed when he was older, how much his mind had retained. At the time it had seemed to leave him untouched, but by some mental osmosis, poems and opinions would float into his mind to match some place or feeling. There were those, sharp-tongued village matrons, who said that the boy had been thoroughly spoilt. But if he had been, then the loving gentle father had equally bequeathed him the self-confidence and independence that made his life a happy game in which he excelled. He needed no life-belt of constant reassurance from other people, neither did he suffer from a conforming mind. Possibly immoral, certainly amoral, Andy Pritchett was a happy, healthy, young man who enjoyed most days of his life.

Pritchett had one more whisky before the landing of the flight from London was announced. As he stood up he glanced around the bar and the restaurant. It was one of his favourite places for picking up new girls. There were few people at that time of night. The flights from Frankfurt and Paris were not due for another hour.

He stood watching through the glass windows as the handful of passengers went through customs and immigration. Anders was one of the first half dozen. He saw him look up, his eyes scanning the arrivals area. He gave no sign of recognition and when he came through the exit doors Pritchett turned and walked towards the street entrance. There was the usual hubbub of people clamouring for taxis, the British distinguishable because they were forming a queue, the Berliners because they were piling into every taxi before it even reached the queue. He waited for the town coach to pass and then walked to the parking lot, threading his way through Mercs and BMWs to a black Volkswagen. He started the engine and sat there waiting. He turned to look for Anders and saw him still standing at the airport exit, reading the front page of a newspaper. Whatever others were doing Anders wasn't leaving things to chance. He was doing what you should do. Waiting to see that all your flight companions had left. A few minutes later Anders looked at his watch, yawned and picked up his bag from between his feet.

As Anders opened the passenger door he heaved his bag on to the back seat.

'Welcome to Berlin, Tad.'

'Thanks. How are things?'

'Much as usual. Except for your thing. I've got a bit more background to give you. How about a meal?'

'Have you eaten already?'

'No. I waited for you.'

'How about we treat ourselves to Kempinski's?'

Pritchett grinned. 'Eat and drink for tomorrow we die, eh?'

'Not if I can help it, friend.'

They had eaten at Kempinski's and then strolled down the Kurfürstendamm and back to Fazanenstrasse where Pritchett had parked his car.

Pritchett's flat was on the top floor of a modern block just to the east of Potsdammerstrasse. The sitting room was comfortably furnished. Very male and very Pritchett. A beautiful nude in *sanguine* by Annigoni had pride of place on the main wall. There were unframed photographs of boats in sunny harbours and girls in bikinis. A row of framed targets with frayed bulls were strung along the top of a set of mahogany bookshelves and a copy of *Playboy*'s German edition was open on the leather couch. There were two clocks on the end of one of the bookshelves. One showed local time and the other looked like Moscow time.

'D'you want a decent night's sleep, Tad or would you rather get working?'

'Let's do a couple of hours, anyway, Andy.'

'I've got the stuff laid out in here.'

They sat side by side at the dining room table, Pritchett with his elbow on the table, his chin cradled in his hand, as he looked sideways at Anders.

'You don't look all that bright, Tad, are you OK?'

'I'm fine.'

'Maybe we should leave this junk till tomorrow?'

'No, I'm OK.'

Pritchett reached out and pulled a small pile of photographs towards them.

'There's the lovely boy himself. Vasili Pavlovich Burinski. Middle to late thirties. There he is again, coming out of the block where he lives. There he is with his wife. He works from an office in the Intelligence block in Normannenstrasse. I can show you a whole pile of photographs of that block. Inside and out, aerial views, architects' plans, the lot. But I suggest you keep well away, the surveillance there is red hot.

'Then four or five shots of him in the street. A bit grainy but he's recognisable. The blue file is four days' surveillance but it doesn't tell you much. He's KGB. I'm not sure of his rank but it's not more than captain. The buff file is accumulated background on him from routine sources. Nothing very exciting, except that he not only did a *Spetsburo* course but seems to have stayed with them. I don't know why you and London are interested in him but I'd say he's a pretty tough cookie.'

'Does he have any personal protection, surveillance or anything like that?'

'Not that's been seen, but it hasn't been a thorough surveillance on our part. You know that, don't you?'

Anders nodded. 'How about Willi Kraus? Is he going to be cooperative?'

'Yes. He's obviously a fan of yours. He's got a car that will get you out of Berlin and another at Magdeburg. He's going to respray and renumber the first one and drive it back to Berlin himself. He's really putting his head on the chopping block for you.'

'What about the set-up in Goslar?'

Pritchett shrugged. 'They're very touchy as you know.'

'Touchy? On what grounds, for God's sake? They're put there to do a job.'

'I know. But they complain all the time that we're overdoing it. When they first set it up things were a lot different. There was more discontent in East Germany. More poverty and more hatred of the Russians and the puppet government. That's all changed. They're comparatively well off now. They still hate the Russians but they've learned how to deal with them. And the penalties for frontier guards are really tough now. Mandatory death sentences if there's hard evidence.

'Ten years' ago we were bringing through four or five bodies a week. About two a month is all we can do now. The Goslar unit has politicals as its main remit, and sticking in another body, two with you, puts the whole programme back a month or more.'

'Nicholson's gone into all that and he gave orders that we had top priority.'

'I know. But up to yesterday they were still protesting that you should use a chopper or bring him through the Wall. That's the usual way out for our East Berlin bodies.'

'What was Nicholson's reaction to the protests?'

'He gave them a flea in their ears. A direct order, but he gave them authorisation to charge it to general funds.'

'How much does it cost these days?'

Pritchett smiled. 'It's not like the old days, Tad, when a couple of hours in the cabin with the girl and a hundred dollars could get half a dozen bodies across. Have a guess at what it costs now?'

'I've no idea. Tell me.'

'Well, for a start you have to cover three men now. East German frontier guards are never the same two men together. There's always a shift between the two being on together again. So three is the smallest number we need to be sure. And even then we have to rely on two days to get someone over. It's a basic three hundred dollars a week for each guard. And a thousand bucks each for every crossing. And girls are thrown in by the dozen.'

'The unit has agreed though?'

'Of course. They take their orders from Nicholson.'

'What contact do I have with them?'

'Willi Kraus knows the drill. Goslar have got a man in Magdeburg, an agricultural machinery salesman, and he'll take you to a farm in a small place called Tanne right on the border. You'll be there one night. Two at the most.'

'Do you liaise with the document section?'

'Yes.'

'I want them to check all my documents and make sure they're OK and up to date.'

'Give them to me when you turn in and I'll take them across myself and they can do them during the night.'

'I'll have tomorrow here to get acclimatised and then go over the next morning.'

'Fine. Let's have a drink before you turn in.'

It was just after one o'clock when Anders pulled the duvet up to his shoulders and he was asleep almost immediately. But an hour later he was awake. He got slowly out of bed and walked to the window, pulling the curtains aside. The apartment block was high enough for him to see across to the Tiergarten.

Despite the lateness the lights of the city were still bright enough to be reflected on the low-lying clouds. Just beyond the black silhouette of the treetops in the Tiergarten he could see the floodlights on the golden figure of the Winged Victory and there were lights on the huge edifice of the Brandenburger Tor. There were fewer lights on the other side of the wall. There were lights at Check-Point Charlie but the barriers were across on both sides. There was a jeep by the Allied control post and a big Merc with a flag on its bonnet. It was too far away to see what flag it was.

Anders was at home in Berlin, he had always been successful on Berlin operations. And he liked the Berliners who lived permanently on the edge of disaster but still found the courage to defy the Soviets and poke fun at the Allies who were there to defend them. They knew all too well that Berlin was not defensible against a Soviet or East German attack: their only real defence was that such an attack would mean World War III had started. They didn't dwell on the likelihood of that disaster. It hadn't been all that many years since Berlin had been a heap of rubble, yet now, a trifle theatrically maybe, they lived successfully on the tightrope. Perhaps the only thing that depressed Berliners was the Wall. Ugly, man-made, it epitomised the differences between the East and the West. Not just the contrived differences of politics and economics but the real and fundamental differences between two kinds of people. Some said it only represented the difference between two sets of rules and that the people were much the same. But, without dwelling on it, most people felt that the differences were total and eternal.

Anders, because he had a Slav background but a western upbringing was often asked what the fundamental differences were, and he had no answer. But he knew that the Wall was a genuine and realistic monument to those differences. It depressed him, and Check-Point Charlie depressed him most of all. He knew its mechanics inside out. He had been through it, both ways, scores of times. Legally and illegally. There was no element of fear in his revulsion. But despite its floodlights Check-Point Charlie looked like a black hole to Anders, a void that led down into the earth, out of the real world into nothingness.

He leaned forward, resting his forehead on the coldness of the window, his eyes closed. And he wished that he was somewhere else. In the club in Soho, in the small house in Morpeth, chopping logs for firewood in the small back-yard. There must be some other work he could do. Something ordinary like other men did. But he groaned because he knew that all that he was good at were the things that he did. He turned sharply as he heard Pritchett's voice.

'What is it, Tad? What's the matter?'

'What do you mean?'

'I heard you talking so I came in. Is there anything I can do?'

'No. I'm OK.'

But Pritchett switched on the light and walked over to him putting his hand on Anders' arm.

'Lie down, Tad. Just rest if you can't sleep.'

He led Anders to the bed and watched, concerned, as he lay back. Pritchett sat on the edge of the bed.

'Do you want me to phone London and get them to call the operation off until you're fitter?'

'No. I'm OK, Andy. Just a fit of the blues.'

'Anything special?'

'No. Like I said, just a passing fit of the blues.'

'I know the feeling.'

Anders turned his head to look at Pritchett. 'I can't see you getting the heebie-jeebies, Andy.'

'Why not?'

'You're not that kind of guy.'

Pritchett half-smiled. 'You think I'm too dumb to have doubts?'

'I didn't mean that.'

'What did you mean?'

'You're all of a piece. You know what you're doing and you get on with it and enjoy it.'

Pritchett laughed softly. 'Those are almost the exact words Peter Nicholson used about you when he was briefing me on this operation. But I wouldn't expect him to understand about you or me. He's a desk wallah, not an operator.'

'So what gives you the blues?'

'God knows. I don't often get that way. No more than I guess you do. But every now and again. I can't remember where I am or why I'm there. And when it all comes back I wish I was somewhere else.'

'Where do you wish you were?'

Pritchett smiled. 'There's this garden. A country garden. Lawns and herbaceous borders and a wooden bench under an apple tree. And there's a girl walking towards me in a dress with flowers on. I don't have any idea what she looks like except that she's breathtakingly beautiful and she's my wife. She's holding a little girl's hand and the little girl's name is Emma. She's our daughter. And there's a brown labrador dog. Fade to music. Vera Lynn singing "We'll meet again". Produced and directed by Andrew Pritchett in conjunction with Thames TV and SIS.'

Anders leaned up on his elbows, smiling, shaking his head. 'And I'd have bet my last dollar that your idea of heaven would be screwing the chorus of the best musical in town.'

Pritchett laughed. 'That ain't a dream, Tad, that's grim reality. And most of the time I like my reality. So do you, you stupid sod. You're just a bit worse than the rest of us because you've got that Slav blood in your veins.' He looked at Anders and winked. 'Get to sleep, honey-chile and dream about those pretty hookers who float around your club.'

Anders nodded. 'OK.' And he nodded again. 'Thanks for the revelations.'

'That's OK. See you later.'

Nicholson stirred in his sleep and then opened his eyes. There was moonlight at the windows and somewhere far away the telephone was ringing. He leaned up on one elbow, testing the moral fibre of the caller. There were ten double rings before it cut off in mid-ring.

Fleur's face was turned towards him, her head back on the pillow, a thick swatch of long blonde hair curved over her shoulder to where her hand lay loosely at her neck. She was frowning in her sleep as if sleeping required the same intensity of effort that she gave to everything else that she did. Then the telephone started again.

There was enough moonlight in the hall not to need to switch on the light and he sat on the bottom stair and reached for the phone. It was Pritchett.

'Where are you calling from, Andy?'

'Berlin. My flat.'

'What can I do for you?'

'I'm worried about Anders, and this operation.'

'Why?'

'First of all I don't think it's been properly assessed. It's too chancy. Too hit and miss. It needs far more back-up than it's getting.'

There was a long pause. 'You may be right, Andy, but it's all we can give it at the moment.'

'So postpone it for a week or two.'

'We can't do that. You know the circumstances. We've promised Bonn to give our friends a bloody nose and we've got to do it . . . You said "first of all". What else is there?'

'I don't think Anders is in the right mood for going over.'

'What on earth does that mean?'

'He's not on top form.'

'You mean he's ill?'

'No. Jesus, it's hard to describe. You need to be all wound-up and raring to go to be successful on these sort of trips. And he's not. He's discouraged.'

'About what?'

'Nothing specific. Just things. His batteries are down.'

'Has he complained, or what?'

'No. He's not the complaining type.'

'There's nothing wrong this end, so far as I know.'

'It's nothing to do with things being wrong, Peter, it's . . . oh God, how can I explain . . . I think you people take him too much for granted. He's on his own in that bloody club. You use him and the club when it suits you but he isn't in the swim. He doesn't get promotions. Nobody's responsible for his morale. He's not made part of the team, the club.'

'He *isn't* part of the club, Andy. It's a pity, but that's how it is. We can't wet-nurse a grown man. Anyway, knowing Anders he'd probably tell us to get stuffed.'

'So what? It's the job of senior people to look after the understrappers.'

'So what do you want me to do? I can't postpone it, that's for sure. Is there anything else I can do?'

'Maybe not right now, but when he's back keep alongside him. Not just when you need him. He's not a bloody gorilla.'

Nicholson said softly. 'What's that mean?'

'I'll have to go, Peter. I've got things to do.'

'OK. Keep in touch.'

Nicholson sat on the stairs looking across the panelled hall. He could just see the reflection from the windows on one edge of the gilt frame of the painting of his father in his judge's wig and robes. Maybe Pritchett's protests were as much on his own behalf as on Anders'. There was always some moaning and groaning from field operators. Sometimes justified, but more often not much more than routine petulance against those who, as they saw it, sat safely in offices moving the pieces around the board. It was understandable. If you were the pawn sacrificed in some early gambit you didn't cheer the ultimate check-mate no matter how subtly it was achieved.

He looked at his watch. It was five o'clock and the moonlight had darkened into the faint summer dawn. He would spend some time with Anders when he was back. It always looked as if Pritchett and Anders led easy-going Bohemian lives that were to be faintly envied rather than pitied. Anders was outside the magic circle but nobody emphasised the fact. Perhaps they did, unconsciously, draw an imaginary line between gentlemen and players but it wasn't intentional and it wasn't the result of official policy. And Pritchett was on the establishment so he had no reason to feel that *he* was out in the cold. He would discuss it with French or maybe Meynell. He stood up, cursed softly as his foot slid on a rug on the polished floor, and walked through to the kitchen and switched on the lights.

It was warm enough to walk out and drink his coffee on the bench in the garden. It was going to be a fine day and people were coming for the weekend. People they both liked. Successful people with no axes to grind, who did things that were worthwhile doing. He had been so lucky with Fleur. Not just beautiful, but alive and capable, running the house and family with French efficiency. Demanding of everyone except of him, because for her he could do no wrong. Please God let it all last. Let nothing go wrong. Let no child be struck down. We do no harm to anyone, let none happen to us. He smiled to himself. It sounded like the prayers he said when he was a small boy. But he realised now that he owed his happy childhood more to his parents than to God. Not ostentatiously loving but always observant and instantly aware of subdued spirit or a shadow on a face.

He remembered the long pieces in the Sunday papers about his father. The terror of the Old Bailey. The judge who addressed the hardest criminal as 'Mister' and explained carefully and scrupulously why he was being sent down for the maximum number of years, as if he were sure to be interested in how the decision was arrived at and the subtle beauty of the law. And the same man bending to listen, wiping the sweat from his face after a set of tennis, intent on what the child was saying. A pause to consider what had been said, then 'Well Peter, that's an interesting problem. What you have to look for is justice. You and Michael agreed to share, and now he refuses and says that it was unfair. Was it? You have an agreement, but *was* it fair? He's two years yonger than you. Did he really understand what he was agreeing to? Did you, perhaps, know things that he didn't know because he was younger? Or is he just a bad loser trying to back off from his word? Think about it, boy. The law of contract or natural justice. An interesting problem. I know you'll enjoy solving it. Let's have a look at the raspberries and see if that netting has worked.'

He never tried to ape his father with his own family but he instinctively used what he had learned as a boy in a happy family, and when he failed with the three girls Fleur succeeded. Not with logic or appeals to fair play but a mixture of Lycée strictness and taking advantage of being loved and admired. She was a gem, a treasure.

Chapter 9

ANDERS WAS up at seven and the world seemed normal and sunny again. The few hours rest, or something, had chased his depression away.

After breakfast he went over the route to Magdeburg and Tanne again on the maps, and read through the background files on Burinski. Pritchett went across for his documents.

The information in Burinski's file was sparse but he sounded like a typical KGB hit-man. The only hard fact was that the journalist, Panov, had sworn that Burinski was the man who had killed the Jugoslav. But Burinski was a common enough name. Was this Burinski the right one? He matched Panov's description: his KGB background and training also fitted; and there were minor descriptive details from two or three unsolved political murders in West Germany that also fitted. The fact that Panov had said the assassin was the son of a Red Army general seemed to make the identification conclusive.

The surveillance sheets only indicated how difficult a kidnap was going to be. Burinski was only on the street when he went to his office and when he returned home. The rest of the day he was in his office, and once home there appeared to be no evening visits. Only once in four days' surveillance had he emerged during an evening, and that was for a matter of minutes when he walked to the corner of the street and posted a letter.

With only two opportunities a day for a pick-up the choice was simple but against all normal tactics. Although a morning pick-up with all the daylight hours for the getaway had advantages, in Burinski's case it was out. His non-appearance at his office would be noticed immediately. It would have to be the afternoon, and that meant driving after dark when there was less traffic on the roads and road-blocks were not visible in advance.

He would watch Burinski himself tomorrow and check the timings, and the next day would have to be the day. It was a Friday, and Burinski's weekend movements had not been under surveillance. And almost certainly he would be expected by his wife and the alarm would be given right away. Anders needed at least twenty minutes to get clear of the city. They would not suspect a kidnapping until they had gone through all the standard routines for delayed husbands: shopping, meetings, girlfriends on the side, hospital checks and arrest records at local police stations. And once kidnapping was a possibility for a man like Burinski they would go for the obvious way out, the Wall. Simultaneously they would be checking his flat for evidence of possible defection. If he was lucky they could be in Magdeburg before the hunt was really on.

Then Pritchett was back with the documents.

'All OK, Tad, but they've put in a couple of extras.' He pushed two pieces of paper across the table. 'This one is a new requirement for visitors to areas within twenty miles of the border. It covers all three of you and it's valid for thirty days from yesterday. This is a medical card covering Burinski in case you decide to drug him. Classifies him as an epileptic sometimes requiring sedation. The card gets you drugs on an emergency basis. Not for you to use but to explain why he's under sedation. They say the rest are first-class and half of them are genuine.'

'Thanks. I'm going through Charlie with one of the guided tours at eleven. I'll be back about four.' He smiled as he stood up. 'I just want to sniff the breeze.'

Pritchett smiled. 'I hope you're not going through with that bulge under your arm. They've got metal detectors on all the time.'

'I'll leave it in the thing beside my bed.'

'I'll put it in my safe.'

Anders went through Check-Point Charlie with the other tourists from the travel agency. The courier collected their passports and fifteen minutes later the coach was through and turned into Friedrichstrasse. They covered the usual sights of the TV tower, Marx-Engelsplatz and Alexanderplatz. And then they had the usual free hour for shopping, with the coach parked at the Brandenburg Gate. He walked up Unter den Linden, took a coffee at a pavement table and afterwards strolled up to the bookshop. It was there, right in the centre of the second row of books. A secondhand copy of Lukàcs' *Geschichte und Klassenbewusstsein.* The original 1923 edition. And the card with the handwritten price – seventeen Ostmarks. He walked slowly back to the coach and chatted in English to the driver about the problems of driving licences and petrol supplies in the Democratic Republic.

It was mid-evening when Pritchett came back. He had that day's surveillance report on Burinski and nothing had changed. Burinski had left his office at 17.05 and had gone into his flat at 17.21. He had been carrying a leather briefcase, an evening paper, and an unidentifiable package.

They ate at Café Wien and then went to see *Kramer v Kramer* at the Astor. Not being fathers they were less moved than the majority of the audience and were unconvinced about ladies who fought legal battles and then gave back the prize money. But a couple of hours in the Black Horse put things back in perspective. Andy Pritchett was at home because he was obviously a regular, and Anders felt at home working out the profit margins. But they were both in demand by girls for dancing, and were experienced enough to turn aside a wide repertoire of propositions without incurring wrath or wounding maidenly pride.

The walked back to the flat in good spirits and were sound asleep just after midnight.

Anders paid the 6.50 marks for his visa, bought his compulsory ration of Ostmarks and was passed through the check point. He had nothing except the clothes he stood up in and he bought a shirt and a spare pair of socks at an

Intershop before taking the S-bahn to the Lichtenburg Station. It took him fifteen minutes to find Burinski's block in Rüdigenstrasse and he timed the walk to the MfS headquarters in Normannenstrasse. Despite the sunshine it looked more like a prison than offices, a dark brown concrete structure with its windows set in long monotonous rows. He only glanced at it as he walked by but he wondered why they had allowed the down-pipes to be mounted on the front of the building. An invitation to break-ins, but maybe the surveillance was too good to tempt anyone to try. There were four uniformed men just inside the big glass-panelled doors.

There was a church in a small square on Burinski's usual route and that was where he'd pick him up. There would be long shadows in the late afternoon from the church itself and from the trees in the churchyard, and the car could wait on the south side and come round as soon as Burinski crossed the square. Then a half circle and straight down the main road to the underpass at Biesdorf.

There was a taxi on the stand by the Rathaus and he took it to the main Ostbahnhof station. He walked inside the station. It was crowded with people and there were long queues at the ticket stations. He looked at his watch. It was midday. There was something odd and he couldn't think what it was. He went back to the station entrance and waited at the lights until they changed. Crossing the street he walked slowly down Mühlenstrasse and turned left. He could hear the siren blasts of barges on the river and at the bridge he saw the Germans-only checkpoint at Oberbaumbrücke. Twenty minutes later he walked past Willi Kraus's workshop. It was up a cobbled yard between two warehouses, a battered notice said W KRAUS AUTO REPARATUREN. Anders walked on up to the corner of Rudolfstrasse and turned to look back. He could hear the roar of traffic in the main street the other side of the warehouses, but in Warschauer Platz itself there was only a youth on a bicycle and a girl with a pram. He stood there for about ten minutes before walking back and turning into the cobbled yard up to the corrugated iron doors. A small door with a battered brass knob was let into the main door, and he turned the knob, opened the door and bent his head and lifted his leg to go through the small opening.

The garage was silent and empty, and there was only a faint light from the long, dirt-encrusted windows on the far wall. In the far corner he saw the glow of a coke fire in a brazier with a crude metal canopy above it. He pushed the door to behind him and walked into the building, his footsteps echoing from the metal roof. There was a small glazed-in office in the far corner and he made his way slowly past stripped down car engines and a litter of spare parts.

The office was empty but when he touched the cigarette butt in the ashtray it was still warm. He stood half inside the office doorway looking around the garage, his eyes more accustomed to the dim light. Willi Kraus was standing behind the small door at the entrance. Smiling, a big wrench held loosely in his hand. He reached out his arm and the lights came on. He turned, opened the small door, looked out and then closed it, turning the key in the lock. He walked over still smiling, his hand held out.

'Good to see you again.'

'Good to see you too. Where do you want me?'

Kraus nodded towards the office. Inside, he moved the old-fashioned swivel chair to one side, pulled back the threadbare greasy carpet and reached down. He tugged twice and then a square of the floorboards swung up with a waft of dank, stale air. There was a steel ladder that went down vertically into the darkness.

Kraus laughed softly, 'It's not as bad as it looks but it isn't the Hilton.' He took a rubber torch from his desk. 'Take this and go on down. I'll close this up when you flash the torch. I'll be down in half an hour.' He smiled. 'Make yourself at home.'

The square hole was barely big enough to take Anders' broad shoulders and the torch in his hand made the descent more difficult. He estimated that he was ten feet down when his feet met the concrete base. He flashed the torch and as the cover swung down overhead he shone the torch on each side of him. The door was at his back and he reached behind him awkwardly to open it. As it opened a light came on and he heard the soft purr of an air-conditioner. He turned his body slowly and entered the underground room.

The room was larger than he expected, about eight feet by six feet. There was an ex-Wehrmacht camp bed and canvas wash-basin, a cane arm-chair, a small table with a battery radio and two small white cupboards hung on the wall. An electric boiling ring and a small heap of crockery and cutlery were on a metal shelf over the bed. The walls, floor and ceiling were concrete roughly painted white, and in the far corner of the ceiling was a white plastic grille over the air-conditioner; a wire trailed down loosely to a plug and socket near the floor. Despite the air-conditioning the walls and ceiling were covered with droplets of condensation, and apart from the dankness there was a smell that he recognised but couldn't identify. A faintly acrid smell.

The cane chair creaked as he sat down. There were two or three paperbacks on the small table and he looked through them and picked one out. It was an Ed McBain, *Würger an Bord*. It was almost an hour before Kraus came down to join him. He had a cellophane-wrapped parcel of sandwiches tucked inside his jacket.

'We'd better eat, Tad. We shan't get much chance tomorrow.' He put the sandwiches on the table. 'Help yourself, I'd better let Pyramid know you're here.' Pyramid was Pritchett's code name.

Kraus knelt down and reached under the camp-bed to bring out a battered leather case, and when he lifted the lid Anders saw the neat black transceiver. It was an Israeli Elta, a model he hadn't seen before, with an LED display and a neat rubber hand-mike. And as Kraus switched on the set Anders recognised the elusive smell. It was ozone generated by the radio set that the small air-conditioner hadn't dispersed. Pritchett responded immediately and

Kraus just said 'Cairo OK.' Pritchett acknowledged and that was it.

Anders went over the timetable and plans for the next day and they turned in just after eight. Kraus insisted that Anders took the camp bed, and slept himself in the wicker chair with his feet on the table. They both slept soundly and Kraus woke Anders at five o'clock. At six Kraus left to pick up the car.

By 7.30 they had driven to the church and Anders had shown him where he wanted the car and then they had parked the car two blocks away and walked back on foot. As if to a timetable, Burinski came out of Schottstrasse and passed the church without even glancing at Anders or Kraus. He had nodded to a woman who passed him and then he was over into the bottom end of Normannenstrasse. There was no difficulty in identifying him: he was exactly like the descriptions and the photographs.

Anders made no attempt to follow Burinski and they walked back to the car and drove back to Kraus's place. Anders took the S-bahn back to Friedrichstrasse and strolled down to Unter den Linden. The book was still there in the window but he walked on, bought a paper and took a table at one of the cafés. He was tempted by the *hühnersuppe* on the menu but hot liquids never went well with the tension of an active operation. He stuck to coffee and toast. Better an empty belly than a queasy one.

He paid his bill and looked at his watch as he waited for his change. It was 1.15. The notice on the bookshop door said that it was closed for lunch from 1 until 2. He reached out and pressed the brass bell button twice. One short and one long. His initial in Morse. There were no lights on in the shop and it was several minutes before he saw the old man's solemn face as he pulled back the bolts and turned the key. He opened the door slightly, Anders said softly, '*Abschied*,' and the old man nodded, his face impassive as he responded. '*Servus*.'

As Anders walked into the shop the old man walked past him into a small section that was curtained off. When he came out a few minutes later he was carrying a small plastic airlines bag with the logo of Berolina Travel on its side. The old man dumped it unceremoniously on the counter and looked up at Anders' face. 'It's heavier than it looks, friend.'

'How is she, Max?'

'She's still in hospital.'

'What's the prognosis?'

The old man shook his head slowly but didn't reply. He touched Anders' shoulder gently as he let him out of the door. 'Thanks for remembering.'

There were half a dozen taxis at the Brandenburger Tor. He let the first one go and took the second to the Oberbaum Bridge and walked the rest of the way back to Kraus's place. The BMW was already in the cobbled entrance facing the right way.

They went over the Berlin street map again to cover the two alternatives. Either way they had to do almost a complete half circle of the city and most of it was on the autobahn. They decided to stick to their original plan and take the long route and turn off the autobahn to Beelitz and use the secondary roads to Magdeburg and then the twisting minor roads bypassing Quedlinburg and up the mountain road to Tanne. But the man in Magdeburg would know the safest route.

Anders gave Kraus the forged identity card, the travel passes, petrol coupons, zone pass and worker's holiday pass for the Trades Union recreation centre at Wernigerode. Kraus had bought a used spare tyre in addition to the spare wheel and Anders slid the canvas bag into the cavity of the tyre. And then it was time to go.

He allowed fifteen minutes for traffic delays and they arrived four minutes early. Anders waited in the car on the south side of the church, breathing deeply and evenly, then, with his hand on the car door he said, 'When you see Burinski, wait until he's half way across the square, count five seconds, and come round. Open the back door as wide as it will go as soon as you're alongside me, and the second I'm inside put your foot down until we're out of the square. Leave him to me no matter what's happening. Understood?'

Kraus nodded and Anders got out and walked the long way round the churchyard. As soon as he turned the corner he saw Burinski and he slowed until Burinski started crossing the square. He heard the car engine start and the squeak of the shock absorbers as it moved. Then it was as if they had rehearsed it a dozen times. As the car came alongside him Burinski turned to look, the rear door was open and in one movement Anders had pinioned the Russian's arms and they fell together into the rear of the car. Burinski went in backwards and his head took a crack from the roof of the car, but he put up his knee to fend off Anders. As the car moved off Anders felt the door against his foot which was still outside and he knelt on Burinski's groin to quieten him as he swung his foot inside. The Russian's head was half under the front seat, his face contorted with pain, and Anders grabbed at the lapels of the man's jacket, bunching them together tightly at his throat.

'Don't move or make a noise, Burinski. I don't want to hurt you.'

The Russian turned his head but couldn't move it from under the metal seat frame. His eyes were hard with anger and he said. 'Whoever you are, you must be out of your mind. You're going to suffer for this.'

Kneeling on Burinski's chest Anders reached in his pocket for the adhesive tape. 'Don't worry, comrade. It's your turn first so keep nice and quiet.'

He saw the shock on Burinski's face as he spoke in Russian not German and he reached forwards and spread the tape firmly across Burinski's mouth. Turning him on one side he roped his hands behind him and then roped his legs.

As he sat back on the seat they were just approaching the Post Office on Strasse der Befreiung. Anders saw a big black Mercedes come hurtling out of the side street. Kraus frantically spun the wheel and then the police car came up from behind hitting them at full speed, turning them sideways until they smashed into the black Mercedes. Then two cars skidded to a halt alongside them and uniformed men poured out. As the rear door was wrenched open, Anders had only a fleeting sight of the club before it struck the base of his skull.

Chapter 10

THE OFFICE was small, with a desk pushed back against the wall. There were two men looking at him: a tall man in civilian clothes and an older man in a KGB uniform.

Ander's hands were handcuffed to the chair behind his back and an ache at the base of his skull throbbed with pain to the beat of his heart.

'What's your name?'

'It's on my documents.'

The tall man closed his eyes. 'What's your name?'

'Anderson'

'Forename.'

'Theo.'

'Have you any explanation to offer for your hooliganism?'

Anders shook his head.

'Who sent you?'

Anders sat silently, his eyes deliberately unfocused. The civilian had spoken German but the KGB man used Russian.

'Kraus has already told us what we need to know.'

Anders looked down at the floor. It was a ritual he knew so well. They were waiting for him to ask why they were questioning him if they already knew everything. Anything to get him talking. It was a standard ploy. As old as the hills, and it never worked with professionals.

When he looked up, the tall civilian was leaning back lazily against the wall, his arms folded, half-smiling as he looked at Anders' face. He spoke very quietly.

'Anders, Tadeusz Anders. SIS officer. And they send you in like a lamb to the slaughter. Why, Anders? What have you done that they want to throw you away? And poor Kraus and the old man, Steiner, at the bookshop. His wife dying slowly in hospital. Which one of you do they want to get rid of? Closing your eyes won't change the facts, my friend.'

The tall man nodded to the KGB man who unlocked the handcuffs from Anders' wrists, put them in his pocket and left the office. The tall man stretched out a long leg, hooked his foot round the leg of a wooden chair and sat down.

'My name's Kalin, Anders. Colonel Kalin, KGB. If we can talk together in a civilised fashion we can bear that in mind when you come up for trial.' He paused and looked with raised eyebrows at Anders' face. 'You've committed almost every criminal act in the book except rape.' He sighed theatrically. 'If you and I can't talk here in Berlin I'll have to send you to Moscow.' He shrugged. 'You don't need me to paint a picture of what happens to non-talking foreign agents in the Lubyanka. It isn't quite as crude as it used to be but modern technology is just as painful and far more efficient. You'll talk in the end, but it's up to you how long it takes.'

Anders stared back at Kalin but said nothing. The Russian sat there silently, watching Anders' face. It was almost five minutes before he spoke again.

'There's no point in wasting time, Anders. I might as well send you to Moscow and let them get started. It is genuinely a matter of indifference to me. If you'll talk with me, well and good. If you want to do it the hard way, so be it.' He looked at the thin gold watch on his wrist. 'I'll give you five minutes Anders. If you haven't started by then, I shall press the bell and that will be that. Understood?'

Anders closed his eyes and fought the urge to touch the ache in his neck. His eyes were still closed as he heard the Russian stand up and take a few paces, and a few minutes later two armed guards in East German army uniforms pulled him up out of the chair and walked him down the empty corridor to a heavy-duty lift. He counted eight floors before the lift stopped and then he was in a brightly lit corridor with cells on each side. He was shoved into number 17 and keys turned in the heavy locks outside. There was a ceiling light in a metal frame and a bed with one blanket, and a bucket in one corner. And then the light went out. He had no idea what time it was. He guessed that he hadn't been unconscious for more than an hour. But it didn't really matter.

The next morning he was given four slices of sausage and a small piece of stale bread, and an hour later the cell door opened and Kalin stood there looking more like an actor than a KGB man. Elegant blue suit, a white shirt and a white tie, and a strong smell of aftershave.

Kalin stood there looking at Anders' unshaven haggard face and he noticed the arrogant, defiant eyes. He opened his mouth to speak, then shook his head and turned away.

Two hours later Anders was at Gatow under escort, and the car avoided the terminal buildings and circled the airfield. It stopped alongside a plane and one of his escorts pointed to the almost vertical metal steps that led into the aircraft.

It was a small military transport plane and all the seats were occupied by troops from an artillery unit going to Moscow on leave. One or two glanced in his direction but a sergeant had spoken to them and obviously warned them off.

Anders' hands were separately handcuffed to the metal arms of the seat and once the plane was airborne the guards left him and sat in the empty area behind him. The plane flew very low, constantly changing course and he guessed that the pilot was cooperating with ground defence and radar units in a routine testing of defences. But the low altitude produced a turbulence that made the ninety-minute journey bruising and unpleasant because he couldn't use his hands to brace himself, and it was a relief when the aircraft banked slowly and he could see the airfield below. It was far too small to be Sheremetyevo, Moscow's international airport. The plane lurched and came in slowly and as its wheels touched down he saw the sign. It was the Red Air Force field at Domodyedovo.

The soldiers picked up their gear and clattered down the metal steps and he watched them form up and march off towards the long low buildings. It was almost twenty minutes before the handcuffs were unlocked and he was shoved towards the open door. It was beginning to rain as he stood on the tarmac with the guards and then he saw the black Zil heading towards them from the cluster of airport buildings.

The guards handed over a small linen bag that he guessed contained his documents and then the two KGB men took him over. They sat each side of him on the back seat and only once did they speak, to give directions to the driver when they were held up by traffic at Sadovniki on the outskirts of Moscow. And then they were on Varsavskoje Sosse, with the Moskva river on their right.

Ten minutes later they had crossed the two bridges over the island and once they were on Karl Marx Prospekt he knew where they were going. He had half expected they were heading for the KGB's newer headquarters on the outer ring-road but it was going to be Dzerdzhinski Square and the Lubyanka.

The rain was lashing down as the car pulled up outside the grim building that filled one side of the square and the uniformed men hurried him up the steps to get out of the rain. But Anders knew that getting soaked to the skin was going to be the least of his worries in the next few days.

The room was stark. The whitewashed walls had no pictures, no decoration and there was no furniture apart from four hardwood chairs and the metal chair that was bolted to the floor just off centre.

Anders was surprised that Kalin was already there. Even in uniform he looked theatrical, as if he had just come from a rehearsal of *Der Rosenkavalier*. But the melting brown eyes were a hunter's eyes as he looked at Anders sitting on the metal chair. Kalin sat on a chair facing him and two men stood behind Anders' chair.

'Now, Mr Anders, I suggest you start talking. Tell me who was in charge of your operation and what you were ordered to do.'

Anders sat there in silence and a few seconds later Kalin's

nod was as imperceptible as the nod of an experienced bidder at a Sotheby's art sale. A hand clawed into Anders' hair, wrenching back his head until his body arched to relieve the pain and a solid rocklike fist crashed against the side of his face. He lashed out with his legs and arms, jerking his head from the man's grip on his hair, and half-blinded he reached for a chair and swung it at the two shadowy figures. The heavy iron-tipped boot caught his kneecap and as he fell he heard a man laugh and felt a violent shattering blow against his body, and as he hit the concrete floor another, and another, and then everything dissolved into blackness.

Somewhere far away there were children singing 'What a friend we have in Jesus', and then it faded away and there were the shouts of a drill-sergeant on the square at Catterick and Luther Meynell was wishing him luck, telling him to take care. And there was a star slowly growing bigger until it was a bulb covered by a metal grille and it was in the ceiling above him. And there was a man looking down at him from a long way away.

A hand took hold of him roughly and he groaned as it pulled him to a sitting position and his hand went to the left side of his chest.

'Are you ready to talk now, Anders?'

The voice echoed painfully in his head and he wasn't sure what the words meant but he shook his head slowly and his stomach flexed as the vomit streamed from his mouth. His eyes were closed and he heard somebody curse him in Russian as he sank back against the wall.

It was a normal office. Carpeted and unfurnished with a modern teak desk, a well-polished table, and six matching chairs. There was a bowl of anemones in the centre of the table at the far end. And both Kalin and Burinski were in civilian clothes.

Kalin lit a cigarette and Anders noticed the pack. It was export Benson and Hedges. It was Kalin who spoke first.

'Mr Anders. All three of us are professionals. Experienced, well-trained, well aware of what goes on in our rather special world. But there are rules in our special world and one of the rules is that you don't talk. At least you don't talk for forty-eight hours so that the others in your network can disperse to try and avoid arrest. You've been in our hands for nine days.' He half-smiled. 'And you haven't talked. However, there are other rules and one of those is that you get every last item of information from a captured enemy agent.'

Kalin paused and tapped the ash of his cigarette into the china ashtray and then looked back at Anders.

'We can't afford to admire courage, Mr Anders. However, I want to make a suggestion to you. Answer me one question. Just one. And I'll make arrangements for the old man and Kraus to be released. And when you are brought before the court we will arrange for the charges to be reduced so that your sentence is also reduced. You can expect twenty-five years in a labour camp as things stand. And a public trial. If you cooperate the sentence could be halved. If you cooperated fully of course then even more lenient arrangements could be made. Do you understand?'

Anders sat silent and unmoving. After a minute's silence Kalin said, 'Mr Anders. There is a point when courage becomes no more than chest-beating and flag-waving. Posturing from the theatre. We are none of us heroes, none of us James Bonds, but men doing a job. Your service serves your country, mine serves the Soviet Union. We do our work. We know each other's names and habits. Our training is much the same. We are much the same kind of people. When it is necessary we are ruthless. When it is necessary we use violence. Not only us, but your people too. It's regrettable in human terms, but that is what our masters require us to do.

'Is it really necessary for me to give the orders for more brutality and the special drugs and the latest technical devices? Do you really need to force me to play these games? I assure you that I have no wish to give such orders. If you force me to, then that is that.'

Kalin's big brown eyes were not hard as he waited for a reply. Anders was conscious of the almost tangible silence in the room.

'What's the question?'

Kalin sighed with relief and stubbed out his cigarette. It was a mistake. It had an air of getting down to business. Quiet victory over a gallant loser.

'Just one simple question, Mr Anders.' He paused. 'Why Burinski?'

Anders looked back at Kalin and slowly shook his head. Kalin closed his eyes in theatrical despair but when he opened them they were no longer those melting spaniel's eyes of a few minutes earlier. And his voice was hard with restrained anger when he spoke.

'I don't understand you, Anders. Just one question. Why in God's name are you so stupid? We've got theories, and sooner or later we'll find out the answer.'

'Not from me you won't.' And Anders gasped as speaking sent a surge of pain through his chest.

'Why not? Tell me why not.'

'You know why not, Kalin.'

'Tell me.'

'Nothing you could do or say would make me talk. But if I had considered talking it wouldn't be sitting here with my ribs caved in and my jawbone showing through my skin.'

Kalin smiled. 'And your people never use violence? You yourself never use violence?'

'I'm not objecting to the violence.'

'What, then? What are you objecting to?'

'Because you're stupid, Kalin. You're too used to interrogating frightened Soviet citizens. You're handsome and elegant but under all that, you're just a bloody animal. It hasn't crossed your dim mind that it hurts me to breathe, let alone talk. You're not a professional, Kalin. You're a bully boy.'

A thin red stream of saliva and blood flowed from Anders'

mouth, over his unshaven chin, dripping slowly on to his filthy shirt. His face was grey with pain and his thick beard was matted with dried vomit and blood. And the hand on his knee was trembling violently. But not from fear.

He saw Kalin reach forward and press one of the buttons on the panel on his desk. The two guards came in from the corridor and shoved him out of the door. As the walls and ceiling in the corridor tilted and swung they dragged him back to his cell.

Meynell had cycled over, and French, Peter Nicholson and Pritchett had travelled up together by car.

French had arranged for Mrs Griggs to open up the cottage and prepare sandwiches and a flask of coffee for them. French himself passed round the sandwiches and poured the coffee. Luther Meynell was aware that apart from himself nobody was looking at anyone else. His diagnosis was guilt. They were an odd mixture. Andy Pritchett, who ignored the handle on his Spode cup and looked as if he would have preferred an army mug. Nicholson, who looked as though he wished he wasn't there. Leaning back in his chair, his head turned to look abstractedly towards the window, his coffee untouched after the first tentative sip. And French himself, Sir Arthur. A neat man, checking the cushion on his chair before he sat down, almost more conscious of his responsibilities as host than the purpose of their hastily arranged meeting.

'Well, gentlemen,' French said. 'We all know why we're here. I'm sorry it had to be in such a rush, but there you are.'

'How long have they had him, Arthur?'

They all looked at Meynell. It was a relief to be with someone who wasn't directly involved in the shambles. Meynell was a sound man. He'd got a shrewd mind and he'd been in the business. He wouldn't want to pin it on anyone. Just find a solution.

'We think he was taken almost immediately. Five days and a few hours.'

'Any ideas on how they got on to him so quickly?'

'Not as yet.'

Nicholson interrupted, speaking quietly. 'I'd say it was lack of preparation, Luther. Too much of a hurry and not enough surveillance.'

'What do you think, Andy?' Luther turned to look at Pritchett.

'I agree with what Peter said. It was spur of the moment stuff and maybe Burinski was more important than we thought. The two men I used for surveillance are pretty low-grade, but they were all I had available. The one who passed me most of the information hasn't contacted us for payment. Maybe they spotted what he was doing and picked him up. He'd talk. Or maybe he was already working for them, doubling with us.'

Meynell raised his eyebrows. 'Where is Anders now?'

Nicholson sighed. 'He was in Berlin for two days. We know that for certain. Maybe he was there longer. But we know he's not there now. I've had an indication that he's in Moscow. That fits the usual pattern. It probably means that he didn't talk in Berlin so they've taken him to Moscow for the treatment.'

'Have we made any diplomatic complaints, Arthur?'

'No. It isn't on. We wouldn't do that for an established agent and we certainly can't do it for an unofficial.'

'Can we make an unofficial approach? The lawyer fellow in Berlin, perhaps.'

Pritchett interrupted. 'If you do that and Anders is holding out with his cover story he'd be exposed immediately.'

Nicholson shook his head. 'He must have been caught red-handed, Andy. They don't need any confirmation of what he was up to. All they'll want to know is why we were doing it.' He turned and looked at French. 'I think we *should* make an unofficial approach, sir. I really do. I think we should offer an exchange and I think we should do it quickly. We owe him that.'

'Why, Peter?'

'Because we rushed him into it. We spent days when we should have spent weeks or even months.'

'I agree, sir.'

French ignored Pritchett's words. Oblique criticism from the Deputy Head of the Soviet desk was one thing. Criticism from field agents was another. He looked directly at Nicholson.

'Who have we got, Peter?'

Nicholson rested his head on the back of the chair, his eyes closed as he thought. When he opened his eyes he shook his head.

'Nothing, Arthur. Two who are far too important to trade, and a dozen routine people.'

'Offer more than one, then.' Meynell said.

Nicholson looked at French. 'Do you want me to have a go, Arthur?'

It was several silent minutes before French responded.

'I just don't know. I'll have to think about it. We could be pouring petrol on the blaze. However unofficial it may be they'll use it against us if it suits their purpose.'

'Your phone's ringing, Sir Arthur. Shall I answer it?'

'No thanks, Pritchett. I'll do it.'

French was back in a few minutes. 'It's for you, Peter. The office.'

When Nicholson came back he put a note into French's hand as he walked past him to his chair. French read the note and looked up. 'Gentlemen, Peter's just had confirmation from his people. Anders *is* in Moscow.'

Meynell shifted in his chair. 'I think you should make unofficial contact, Arthur. You needn't mention names or cases. Just dip your toe in and test the water. If it's a blank refusal you've lost nothing. If they're open to talks you could establish a shopping list that doesn't pinpoint Anders. Say four names from each side. Possibles. The usual ritual.'

French turned to Nicholson. 'Will you do that, Peter.'

'Yes, sir.'

Paul Degens looked more like an American than a German. In his middle fifties, he had a big, handsome face and the body of a retired professional sportsman. No longer all muscle, but still heavy and strong. With alert blue eyes, a pleasant sensual mouth and a thick crop of wavy hair, there was a touch of Harvard Business School about him.

In fact he had been a major in a German parachute regiment until he was severely wounded in the attack on Crete. Invalided out of the army he had finished his law training and gone into practice on his own, specialising in company law. The successful practice lasted less than six months when it disappeared with everything else in the cloud of smoke and rubble that was Berlin in 1945. When, in the fullness of time, the first Russian soldier had been tried by a German court for rape, Degens had defended him. Despised by his countrymen, he had defended the Russian ably and successfully. Three months after the 'not guilty' verdict had been passed two things happened that changed the whole of Degens' life. The Russian *Kommandatura* and the East German authorities paid him a six-figure annual retainer as their adviser on German Law, and he married the rape victim.

Two decades later he spoke good English and poor but fluent Russian, and seldom appeared in court except to represent any of the surviving companies who had employed him when he started his first practice.

His office was typical of a successful Berlin lawyer. Expensive, well-made, solid furniture, and the lived-in look that men who work long hours sometimes create. He wore a well-cut mid-grey suit that added to his bulk but didn't detract from his business-like aura.

Paul Degens was the man to whom governments came when they wanted to exchange one prisoner for another. Whether it was a U-2 pilot, a dissident or a spy, Paul Degens was the man you talked to. Provided that the Soviet Union was involved on one side or the other. And like most foreigners who appeared to be trusted by Moscow, and with access to top politicians and the Intelligence services he was less trusted by all the other countries who used his services. He asked for and received no fee for these services, but made no secret of the fact that he was paid a substantial retainer by Moscow and East Berlin as a legal adviser.

Nicholson had dealt with Degens before. He liked him as a man, and found him helpful, tactful and totally discreet. He made no attempt to clothe himself in any spurious authority, neither did he use words like 'intermediary' or 'honest broker'. He was no more and no less than what the facts indicated. A competent lawyer who had access to both sides. He negotiated when it was helpful but he didn't drive bargains, that was up to his principals. Nobody had ever claimed that he had told a lie, exaggerated or misinformed them. He had once made a genuine error to the Russians' disadvantage and they valued him enough to go along with the arrangements he had made.

Degens looked at Nicholson, his hands clasped on his desk, the knot of his tie pulled down from his shirt collar.

'So far as I know they are not indicating any desire to exchange at the moment but I'll check just to make sure.'

'How long will that take?'

'If my contact is available, ten minutes. Otherwise it could take me an hour or two to contact an alternative.'

'Would you be willing to try?'

'Of course. Would you like to wait?'

'If that's convenient to you.'

'Certainly. No, don't get up. I'll get my secretary to bring you a coffee. There are magazines there on the side-table. I'll be as quick as I can.'

The coffee came, and Nicholson browsed through a *New Yorker* and a copy of *Playboy*. It was almost half an hour before Degens came back, closing the door carefully and getting back behind his desk before he spoke.

'It's much as I thought, but they mentioned a Russian named Gorlinski. Andrei Gorlinski. I think they would be interested in talking about him.'

'Is there any way I could indicate interest without naming the prisoner we are interested in?'

'No. I don't want to be involved in a poker game. If both parties start fishing for reactions we end up in a Middle East bazaar situation. The Soviets have responded to you. They've named their interest. You have to do the same if you want to pursue it further.'

'My interest is a man named Anders. He was arrested in Berlin and taken to Moscow. He's in the . . . I guess it doesn't matter where he is. I would exchange Gorlinski for that man.'

Degens slid his hand inside his jacket and pulled out a folded piece of paper. He unfolded it and read it carefully twice. Then he looked up at Nicholson.

'Moscow gave me a list of names of people they would not be willing to consider for exchange. Mr Anders' name is not on that list so it looks as if it might be possible.'

'Do you want me to confirm Gorlinski in writing?'

'No. I assume you have the authority to commit your service or you wouldn't be here.'

'So what next?'

Degens looked at his wristwatch, and then at Nicholson.

'I can phone now, if you wish.'

'I'd be glad if you would.'

Degens smiled. 'That word "glad" always puzzles me. In the dictionary it gives the meaning as *froh* or *erfreut*, but they mean happy or pleased. What's the difference between glad and pleased?'

Nicholson smiled back. 'Glad is a milder word than pleased. Less enthusiastic. A smile but no flag-waving.'

'A word you could use when you didn't want to seem as if you would be very pleased.'

Nicholson laughed. '*Touché*. Very discerning of you to notice. It was instinctive, not deliberate.'

'Of course. But I'm a lawyer and even full-stops and commas matter to me. I may be longer this time. You are welcome to stay, or otherwise we could meet later this evening.'

'I'll stay on. Or . . .'

Degens smiled and interrupted. 'No. You staying does not indicate to the other party or me that you are anxious to finalise the arrangements. The other party will not know, and for me I assume the best. That you are conscientious and that Mr Anders is a colleague of yours. I should be anxious for a man's release if he were a friend of mine.'

It was a shorter wait. Degens was back in ten minutes. And once again he didn't speak until he was sitting behind his desk, as if that was a symbol of truth and straight dealing.

'That's OK, Mr Nicholson. They are agreeable. The exchange would be made here in Berlin in a few weeks' time. Maybe a little longer. I'll pass on the details when I have them.'

'Thank you for your help, Dr Degens.'

'Don't thank me, Mr Nicholson. I'm just a messenger-boy. Where can I contact you?'

'Through the consulate. Ask for Mr Treadgold.'

'Ah yes. I know Mr Treadgold. I expect you are already occupied this evening or I would invite you for a meal.'

'Thank you. I shall fly back tonight.'

'Have a good journey.' Degens held out his hand and Nicholson took it.

'Again, thanks for your help.'

Degens smiled and shook his head as he opened his office door.

Chapter 11

ANDERS LAY lay still on the concrete slab, looking up at the ceiling. There was more light than usual, and he guessed that it must have snowed in the night and it was the reflection from the snow that lit the grey paint on the ceiling, and the dull metal of the circular light that was set into the concrete.

He knew that sooner or later he would have to move, and the pain in his ribs and kneecap was bearable now, but if he moved it would be back like a raging flood and he would be tempted to ask for the morphine. The plaster along his jaw hung down to touch his neck, and the stench from the suppurating wound was still offensive despite the antibiotic; the pain from the open wound pulsed with the beat of his heart. He closed his bloodshot eyes against the light, and lay quietly for several minutes until, without conscious decision, he clenched his teeth and sat up, swinging his feet to the ground. He groaned, his eyes still closed, as the pain in his chest and leg flared up like a forest fire. And as he sat there he heard the steel shutter pushed aside in the cell door. Then the rattle of the heavy keys in the two locks.

Anders opened his good eye to turn to look as someone came into his cell. It was Burinski and he was in his uniform. He looked clean and smart, but uneasy as he walked over towards Anders.

'Are you feeling better?'

Anders didn't reply but his good eye watched Burinski's face intently. Something had changed. He could tell it. Was it a change for the good or were things going to get worse?

'I've arranged for you to be transferred to the hospital. Do you agree?'

Despite the pain Anders managed a half-smile.

'A psychiatric ward, comrade? And a tape-recording that I agreed to go?'

'No. The prison hospital.'

Burinski stood there awkwardly and Anders realised that he was just a messenger boy. Burinski didn't know himself why there was a change of attitude. He was a spaniel bringing a bone, wagging its tail and waiting for a pat on the head.

Then the keys rattled again in the door and a man came in. He was dressed like a doctor. A white coat and a stethoscope round his neck; and a smell of strong disinfectant. But in the Lubyanka Prison that didn't mean he *was* a doctor. It meant only what was visible. A man dressed as a doctor. He stood looking Anders over and then he said with a heavy Georgian accent: 'Are you able to walk?'

Anders nodded, but it was an act of useless defiance. He couldn't walk. He couldn't even stand up. For a moment the doctor stood there and then he walked to the door and spoke through the grille to the guard. When he came back he said to Burinski, 'What injuries has he got?'

'I don't know.'

The doctor gave him a brief look of disgust and turned back to Anders.

'Have you had drugs?'

Anders nodded. 'Morphine.'

'Antibiotics?'

'Two days.'

The pain in Anders chest was spreading and mounting because he had spoken and there were beads of perspiration on his forehead and his cheeks. He was unconscious before the two orderlies came with the wheeled stretcher and in the operating room the doctor carefully cut the clothes from Anders' body. He shook his head slowly as he saw the white rib-bone where it pierced the skin and the huge swelling on the left knee. He sliced and sewed for four hours before Anders was wheeled to a hospital cell.

Anders was kept under heavy sedation for a week but when he finally surfaced he realised that the treatment he had been given had been efficient and effective. On the tenth day the doctor had told him to get out of bed and there had been no more than bearable pain in his chest. Although his knee was not articulating freely the swelling had gone down, and the wound along his jawline was almost healed.

The next day Burinski came to visit him, bringing a couple of English newspapers and that day's *Pravda*. He sat on the edge of Anders' bed and was obviously eager to talk. Was there anything else he wanted? Was he satisfied with the medical treatment? Anders ignored the questions.

'What is it you want, Burinski?'

'I want to help you.'

'Don't bullshit me, comrade, you're wasting your time.'

'Why shouldn't I want to help you?'

'Two reasons, my friend. First of all you've got no reason to help me, and secondly, you haven't got the authority to help me even if you wanted to.'

Burinski looked uneasy and Anders guessed that the conversation was being taped.

'You're being moved in a few days. Outside Moscow. A kind of . . .' Burinski sighed as he sought for the right word, '. . . recuperation. A chance to recover.'

'Why the sudden concern?'

'They're not inhuman, you know. They respect your courage.'

Anders smiled. 'They're wasting their time, Burinski. The soft touch won't work with me. They ought to know that.'

'It will be just you and me. No more interrogation of any kind.'

Anders lay looking at Burinski, wondering why the KGB had seen him as an assassin. There was no doubt that he had murdered the men they had picked as his targets, but there was a flaw in his character, a fundamental weakness under the dedication. They had trained him and used him, but you needed more than that. You needed either conviction or an inborn lust for killing. Burinski had neither. And right now the flaw was showing through. He was under some pressure. There was something they wanted, and it was Burinski's job to get it. Anders wondered what it could be.

The next day Burinski brought clothes for him to wear and a carton of English cigarettes and a lighter. Two days later Burinski brought a leather case and said they were leaving. There had been no formalities, they had just walked to the lift and gone down to street level, along a narrow corridor to the main doors and then they were at the top of the main steps in Dzerdzhinski Square. It was a grey spring day. A Moscow spring day, and although it was mid-morning cars had their lights on and there was frost or light snow on the buildings, and a big black Volga M124 its engine running, at the foot of the steps.

Burinski sat with him in the back of the car as the driver threaded his way through the city. The only thing Anders recognised was Sokolniki Park and he guessed they were heading almost due east. When they crossed the outer ring road the signs said 'Gorenki 5km'. As they turned off the main road they took a road marked 'Balasicha' and at the start of a pine forest they took a rutted road that eventually brought them to a lake. There were half a dozen well-built log houses alongside the lake, and at the far end was a stone-built house with a high wall and heavy iron gates. The gates were opened as they drove up, and inside was a wooden hut on wheels and half a dozen armed soldiers. The gardens were large and well maintained, mainly lawns and well-established trees. A Red Army lieutenant waved them on to the house.

The house itself was smaller than it had appeared from outside and an elderly woman held open the door and bowed her head as they walked inside. Burinski took him up the wide oak staircase and showed him his room. It was spotlessly clean and sparsely furnished with solid peasant furniture. A bed, a chest, a wardrobe, a worktable and two carved arm-chairs. There were bars on the small window.

Not even after a week had Anders discovered the purpose of the changed treatment. Burinski seemed almost as much a prisoner as he was, but on the second Sunday Burinski had surprised him as they walked together in the garden, the snow squeaking crisply as they walked under the bare trees.

'My wife's coming to join us. She's arriving tomorrow.'

'Is she KGB too?'

Burinski sighed. 'No. Anyway, she's German not Russian.'

Anders half-smiled. 'Why don't you come clean, Burinski and tell me what it's all about?'

'I'm not sure what it *is* all about.'

'So what do you *think* it's all about? Why is your wife involved?'

'Oh, that's just me. I hate being away from her. She means a lot to me. It's a favour just to keep me happy.'

'You still haven't answered. What do you think it is?'

'I think they're considering an exchange of prisoners.'

Anders stopped walking and turned to look at Burinski.

'You mean me?'

'Yes.'

'What makes you think that?'

'London offered an exchange almost as soon as we picked you up.'

'I don't believe it.'

'They offered one of our people in exchange.'

'How long have they been negotiating?'

'Ever since we got you.'

'That's why you've been patching me up?'

'Yes. I expect so.'

'Who's holding things up?'

'Nobody. It's just a question of ironing out the snags.'

'What snags?'

'I don't know. I've not been told.

Burinski's wife, obviously pregnant, arrived the next day, and the three of them had eaten their meals together. After a few days Anders realised that for all Burinski's ruthlessness he was the weaker partner in the marriage, obviously very dependent on his young wife. Anders realised too from several remarks that she made that she was not one of Moscow's admirers. She made no open criticism but she had smiled her disbelief at several propaganda items on the TV news. She had a different kind of self-confidence from Burinski's rather macho arrogance. A self-confidence that came from a shrewd, informed mind. He wasn't surprised to learn that she worked in a news office.

On the few occasions when he was alone with her she had asked him no awkward questions. He guessed that she knew that he was a foreigner and under some kind of restraint but she made no attempt to probe. She was a jazz enthusiast and she talked knowledgeably. An Oscar Peterson, Earl Hines fan. She had talked too about her parents and the farm, and what it was like when she was a girl, but he got the impression that the best time in her life was now. She obviously genuinely cared for her husband. There were times when she was almost excusing his rôle, but otherwise her comments lacked the ring of conviction that she usually had with all her views.

Alone in his room at night Anders wondered why SIS had offered to do a deal. They never did that. Once you were in the bag you didn't exist. They'd never heard of you. And even if an exchange took place the initiative always came from Moscow. And right to the bitter end London claimed that their man was no more than an innocent businessman falsely entrapped by the machinations of the KGB. It was odder still to acknowledge a man who wasn't on the establishment. They knew him too well to think that he'd crack and talk. Maybe Meynell had suggested it and put pressure on Sir Arthur. But why? Maybe Burinski was mistaken, or maybe the whole scenario was phoney, a ruse to build him up and then deflate him by the disappointment. Yet by now they'd have some background stuff on him from the Embassy in London and they'd at least know that he wasn't likely to be vulnerable to that kind of ploy. And when the KGB wanted an exchange they usually wanted it over quickly. It seldom took longer than a week from first approach to the final exchange. They must have been negotiating for nearly three months.

From time to time Anders thought about Judy and Candy and the club. They would probably have put in somebody to hold the fort at the club. Joey would be able to look after the day to day running. Candy would be worried, pulling underground strings to find out if he had been spirited away by the police. He had no idea what Judy's reaction would be. It would almost certainly be introspective. She would either see it as a desertion, or proof that her father's warnings about his unsuitability were well-founded. Facing the facts he guessed that it was unlikely that she would worry on his account. For Judy, when one life-boat foundered you looked around for another.

Burinski had gone to Moscow for the day. Anders and the girl walked in the garden in the morning under the watchful eyes of the guards. The snow had gone and there were the first signs of spring. The sky was still grey and the air was cold, but there were thin tentative shoots of new grass on the lawns, and a sheen on the reticulated bark of the silver birches that spoke of the end of the season of dormancy. They lunched together and, as if the burgeoning world outside had touched their spirits, they had been relaxed and the girl had been mildly flirtatious. Not seriously, but as if for the first time she saw him as a man. The old *babushka* had cleared the table but they sat there talking and she had told him a mildly anti-Soviet Berlin joke that made him smile. She looked back at his face.

'You know, that's the first time I've ever seen you smile.'

He shrugged. 'I haven't had much to smile about lately.'

'How did you get hurt?'

He put his finger to his lips to warn her that the room would be bugged.

'I got hit by a car.'

She nodded her understanding.

'Did my husband tell you that I'm pregnant?'

'No. But I noticed. When is it due?'

'End of June according to the doctor.'

'D'you want a boy or a girl?'

'I want a boy like Vasili.' She laughed. 'And he wants a girl like me.' She shook her head, smiling with pleasure. 'I don't really mind. Shall we go for another walk in the garden before it gets dark?'

'Why not? I'll get my coat and meet you in the hall.'

He walked her away from the trees and the wooden benches until they were clear of anything that could conceal a microphone.

'Can I call you Inge?'

'Of course.'

'Don't ever say anything critical or private in an official building, especially a KGB one. They're all wired for surveillance. You're the wife of a KGB officer so you're pretty safe, but it all goes down on your record. It can be used some day if they want to.'

She stood with her hands in her coat pockets, her coat collar turned up and her eyes were on his face.

'Why do you warn me?'

'Why shouldn't I?'

'I think you're a prisoner. You can't possibly care what happens to me.'

'Why not?'

'Why should you?'

'You're a human being. And you don't look like you particularly want to be a martyr.'

'You must be very sure of yourself.'

'Why?'

'To care about anyone else when you're in danger yourself. Especially the wife of your . . . enemy.'

'Your husband's not my enemy. Rival, maybe. The enemy are the men in the Politburo. But they're everybody's enemy. Yours as well as mine.'

'Will it ever change?'

'I shouldn't think so. Not substantially.'

'Will there be a nuclear war in the end?'

'I don't think so. The Kremlin may want to take over the world but they want it all in one piece, just as it is, with everything working, not a radioactive desert.'

She sighed. 'I hope you're right.' She paused. 'Are you married?'

'No.'

'Divorced?'

'No.'

'Girl friend?'

He half-smiled. 'I've not heard from her. Who knows?'

'You don't really like women, do you?'

'I like them a lot. But I can get by without one. I don't rely on them to make my life.'

'Maybe you'll fall one day.' She smiled.

'Maybe. I hope not.'

'That's a terrible thing to say.'

He laughed. 'Why?'

'I don't really know. But it's unnatural somehow.'

'The birds and the bees and the survival of the species?'

'No. Just love and friendship and trust.'

He looked at her face. She was quite pretty. He didn't want to hurt her or spoil her dreams.

'We'd better go back, or the Red Army will be getting agitated.'

They walked back in silence and as they approached the house Burinski's car came through the main gates and the girl waited for him as Anders walked into the house and up to his room. He didn't know it but it was almost the last night he was to spend in the house.

The next day Burinski arranged for them to walk outside the garden of the house, across the fields and up the slope to the woods on the brow of the hill.

At the edge of the woods they found a felled tree trunk and sat together looking across towards the house and the lake. Burinski seemed more relaxed than usual and his wife said, 'Go on, Vasili. Say it.'

Burinski turned to look at Anders. 'I want to thank you for warning my wife against being indiscreet. She's German and she doesn't understand these things.'

'I do, Vasili. I understand all right. What I can't understand is how millions of people tolerate it.' Her voice was insistent.

Burinski smiled. 'We don't think about it. We're used to it. It's like the weather. And ninety-nine per cent of those millions have no complaints against the Party. They complain about shortages but there's no country in the world where the people don't complain about something or other.' He turned to look at Anders. 'Isn't that so, Mr Anders?'

'There is a difference, of course.'

'What's that.'

'Their complaints are listened to. They can throw out the politicians every four years and shortages of food and goods seldom happen. In the Soviet Union it's permanent.'

Burinski smiled. 'You just don't like Russians.'

'Not true. I just don't like the Soviet system. And despite what you say, most Russians don't like it either. They tolerate it because it's a dictatorship and they have no choice.'

'How is it you speak such good Russian?'

'My father was Polish. I found Russian fairly easy. How did you learn your German?'

'School. University and . . . service courses. What does your father do?'

'He's dead. He was in the Free Polish Army. He was killed at Monte Cassino.'

'My father was a career soldier. He's retired now.'

'Where does he live?'

'Just outside Moscow.'

'D'you see much of him?'

'No.' Burinski shrugged. 'We don't see eye to eye on many things.'

'Have they told you to pump me on my background?'

Burinski looked shocked. 'Good God no. I was just chatting. Anyway they've got your background on file.'

'Have you read it?'

'Not all of it. Part of it is restricted.'

'Why are we talking like this? You must have a reason.'

Burinski shrugged. 'No special reason. I was just grateful that you warned Inge.'

'No more than that?'

'They are puzzled about you, and interested.'

'Puzzled about what?'

'That somebody so senior in SIS should have been sent on such an unplanned mission. They wonder why. They wonder if you were deceived in some way.' Burinski looked at Anders' face. 'They have been trying to decide whether it would be sensible to suggest you should be offered a senior rank to work for us. Not against the British.'

Anders half-smiled. 'And what did they decide?'

'That I was to see if you were interested even slightly. If you were then somebody very senior would talk with you. You would be offered at least colonel in the KGB.'

'I'm not interested, Burinski. You'd better tell them that.'

'I told them already that you would not be interested. I think it was their view too. But they insisted I make an approach.'

'Are you permanently in Moscow now?'

'No. When you leave I shall be going back to Berlin with Inge.'

Anders looked past Burinski to his wife. 'I guess you'll be glad to go back.'

She shrugged. 'It's been interesting seeing Moscow but, yes, Moscow makes East Berlin seem like civilisation, and God know it isn't. But when I got to Moscow it was like there was a power-cut or somebody had switched off all the lights.' She put her hand on Burinski's arm. 'We're being unkind aren't we, Vasili?'

'Yes. But I understand. We'll have to get back to the house, my love.'

She linked her arms in theirs and they walked slowly back down the hill. Before they came in sight of the house she put her hands back in the pockets of her coat.

They ate together that evening and watched a sports programme on TV. Burinski, for once, kept to his orders and switched off before the news came on.

For the next three days they walked together away from the house. There had been no more talk of politics or political systems and Burinski had asked him no more questions about his background. It was obvious that Inge was the centre of Burinski's life, and Anders wondered what the girl would think if she knew that her husband was a professional assassin for the regime she so obviously despised. She probably wouldn't believe it when eventually she found out, because you would have to have been in the business to believe it and notice the give-away signs. The eyes that looked around without moving, the quick reflexes, the sudden change from normal body movements to complete stillness, the almost imperceptible holding of his breath as he listened, and the barely controlled swagger as he walked when he was relaxed and at ease.

There was an ornamental iron bench under one of the apple trees and they sat there in the pale spring sunlight after their walk. Burinski had been called to Moscow again.

She turned to look at Anders. 'The scar on your jaw has almost blended into your skin.' She smiled. 'But I'm sure your girlfriend will notice it.'

Anders smiled. 'Maybe.'

'Tell me about her. What is she like?'

Anders looked away towards the house and was silent for several moments. The girl said, 'Have I offended you?'

'No. I was just thinking. I've got two girlfriends and I was wondering which one to describe.'

'Are they both alike?'

'No. They're very different. One is sophisticated. From a well-known family in her own small country. The other is younger, prettier and from a working-class family.'

'Tell me about the sophisticated one.'

'She's married. Unhappily. She's a Roman Catholic. The family are mildly important but not wealthy. They care a lot about public opinion and status and that sort of thing. She's attractive but not pretty. She has a drink problem and maybe a drug problem.'

'What's her name?'

'Judy.'

'And the other one?'

'She's very young and very pretty. Very loving and . . .' he shrugged. '. . . I don't know more than that.'

'But you don't love either of them?'

Anders smiled. 'It's worse than that, Inge. I love both of them.'

'What do you love about the Judy girl?'

'I feel great sympathy for her. She looks as though she's always had everything but she hasn't. They were not loving people, they were cold-hearted and only concerned with appearances. She drinks to escape from thinking about her life. She has no talents, no skills, no means to earn a living. She's alone and quite defenceless.'

For a moment she was silent then she said softly. 'You're a strange man, Mr Anders. You don't understand women, do you?'

Anders half-smiled. 'You tell me.'

'You're a very strong man. Very tough. So strong that you can afford to be loving. Inside you are loving, but for some reason you don't want it to come out. Why?'

Anders shrugged and said nothing.

'Was there a girl before these?'

'Yes.'

'What happened?'

Anders shook his head without speaking. The girl said, 'Some time in your life some woman, some girl, must have hurt you very much. I wonder who it was. And now you have two girls. One who is a lame dog you protect out of sympathy, and one who loves you even though you don't love her back. Maybe some day a man will feel sympathy for the loving girl who is not loved back. Maybe it will be you.'

Anders stood up. 'We should be getting back.'

'Have I offended you?'

'No.'

'Angered you?'

'No.'

'I do it only out of affection and because you cared about me and my husband enough to warn me that I was being stupid.'

'Forget it, Inge. In a sane country it wouldn't be necessary.'

'If I don't have a chance to talk to you again, I hope you are happy when you get back.'

Anders nodded and the girl was disappointed at his lack of response.

He was deeply asleep when they roused him and he woke with a start to see one of the guard sergeants standing by his bed.

'You leave in half an hour, comrade.'

'Where for?'

'Half an hour,' the sergeant said, ignoring the question.

At Sheremetyevo a KGB man in civilian clothes took him over from the two Red Army officers and he was escorted across the tarmac to the big Aeroflot jet. It was still dark and the cabin clock showed the local time as 06.00 hours.

When they landed at Schönefeld there was a car waiting on the apron and an hour later they were making their way through the centre of East Berlin. Except when Anders had needed to use the toilets on the aircraft the KGB man had not spoken a word. At the far end of Unter den Linden he had been transferred to a van. He was put into the back, his left foot handcuffed to his left hand and to a ring on the floor of the van. He had noticed the squat dish-aerial revolving slowly on top of the van's roof and the KGB man had spoken half a dozen numbers into a walkie-talkie before he locked the heavy steel door that left the interior in complete darkness.

For almost ten minutes the van waited and Anders could hear nothing; not even the traffic in the busy street; then the engine started and the van moved off slowly. It made no turn and Anders guessed they must be approaching the Brandenburger Tor. A few minutes later the engine was cut and the vehicle rolled on silently, slowly pulling to the left as it braked smoothly.

Anders heard the van door slam to and then there was

silence again. Slowly his head went down until it was resting on his free arm across his knees; his eyes closed, and he slept.

The KGB man had already unlocked the handcuffs before Anders came to, and when he opened his eyes he saw that the door was open and two Red Army soldiers were standing in the road at the foot of the short metal steps. One of them reached up for his arm as he stumbled on the first step and Anders roughly pushed the helping hand aside. He took a deep breath as he stood unsteadily in the road. It was obviously the early hours of the morning. There were no civilians about and he noticed then that there were no East German *Volkspolizei* or Frontier Police who usually manned the Germans-only checkpoint at the Brandenburg Gate. Apart from the KGB man there were only half a dozen Red Army soldiers, their Kalashnikovs held loosely with the sling looped across one arm.

Then suddenly the lights went on, flooding the whole area where they were standing. The KGB man took his arm and pushed him to the big circle of light where two floodlights merged, and spoke softly into his small transceiver. He paused, listening, then spoke again, and a torch flashed three times from the darkness ahead of them. Still holding Anders' arm he pushed him forward, walking slowly towards the guard hut, and another set of lights came on on the other side of the barrier.

Anders saw the balding head and the wispy hair above Andy Pritchett's belligerent face. A man in a dark anorak stood beside him as they both walked slowly towards the barrier. The KGB man muttered again into his small radio and Anders saw Pritchett doing the same. As he was pushed forward the man in the anorak crossed a few feet away, smiling towards his KGB colleagues.

Anders saw Pritchett's eyes on the scar along his jaw and then he held out his hand. It was cold and damp as Anders took it and Pritchett said softly. 'The green Volkswagen's ours. Keep moving.'

Chapter 12

THEY HAD coffee from a thermos as the driver headed for Tegel, and at the airport they had a meal. As he pushed aside his empty plate Anders said, 'Who's been looking after the club?'

'I have. And Stoppard.'

'How're things?'

'No problems.' He smiled. 'Except your little blonde. She's been raising hell in all directions. And a girl named Judy rang a few times early on.'

Anders nodded. 'Who suggested the deal?'

Pritchett avoided his eyes. 'No idea, Tad.'

'Who briefed you, for instance?'

'Skip it, Tad. Wait till we get back. It's not safe to talk here.'

'You mean the KGB might discover they've let me out.'

Pritchett saw the anger in Anders' eyes but made no effort to placate him.

'Just cool it, Tad. If you want to beef, you've got the wrong guy.'

'Who's the right guy?'

'For Christ's sake, what's the problem? They got you out and that's more than they'd normally do for any of us.'

'Where are we going?'

'London.'

'Where?'

'You'd better wait and see. They'll want to debrief you. I'm not in the picture.'

Then the Tannoy was calling their flight and they walked to the gate.

At Gatwick Nicholson was waiting with a Rover 2000, and Pritchett went off to get his own car from the multi-storey.

Nicholson looked tired but amiable and when Anders asked him where they were going he didn't hesitate. 'Tunbridge Wells.'

The house at Tunbridge Wells was one of SIS's safe-houses. It was one of the big Victorian houses in Broadwater Down. Set in its own large grounds, it was one of the few that had not been turned into four or five large flats. SIS used it for a variety of purposes when top security and physical security were essential. From the outside it looked like the rest of the houses, but inside it was a mass of electronics, recording gear and weapons. A plain-clothes CI section was permanently based at the house. They did one-month stints and were not allowed out of the house in daylight hours.

Anders sat without talking, absorbing the information, working out the implications. They were on the main A21 at Farnborough before he spoke again.

'Who's debriefing me, Peter?'

'I am.'

'How long will it take?'

'Not long I should think. Providing you cooperate.'

'Why was Pritchett doing the strong, silent man bit?'

Nicholson laughed softly. 'Was he? Protocol I suppose. The debriefing officer's privilege and all that.'

'How's the club?'

'God knows, Tad. I wouldn't be seen dead in it. You know that. Not my scene at all. They'll have kept it going, you can be sure of that. But they won't be using it as a safe-house without you being there.'

'Can I make a couple of phone calls?'

'Get some sleep in. Let's have a chat and see how it goes, eh?'

Anders didn't reply. They were by-passing Sevenoaks, and the signs were for Tonbridge and Hastings. As he gazed silently out of the window he could see the light of the false dawn silhouetting the hills to the east. There were few vehicles on the road and they were all heading in the opposite direction, for London. Then they turned off the main road onto the feeder for Tunbridge Wells. Fifteen minutes later they were turning left at the Pantiles into the Frant road and at the top of the hill they turned into Broadwater Down. The safe-house was about three hundred yards up on the left, and Nicholson turned into the gravel drive and parked by the double garage at the side of the house. They both got out, Nicholson reaching into the back seat of the car for his bag, Anders looking up at the pink dawn behind the trees. He looked without thinking at his wrist to check the time and then remembered that his watch had gone in the first few days of interrogation.

'Have you got any kit, Tad?'

'No.'

'Nothing?'

'No.'

'The bastards. Let's go in.'

Anders slept until midday and when he woke he saw that someone must have come down from the club. A suit, some shirts and a pair of jeans were laid out on the other single bed.

He was sitting on the edge of his bed when the phone on the bedside table rang. As he put the receiver to his ear a male voice said, 'Press the scrambler button please, Mr Anders.' He pressed the button and recognised Luther Meynell's voice.

'Welcome back, Tad. How are you feeling?'

'It makes a change to hear somebody say welcome back.'

'Give them time, Tad. I expect they've been mainly concerned with getting you back to London.'

'Was it you who suggested the exchange?'

'It was a joint decision. Is there anything I can do to help?'

'Maybe I could come up and see you for a couple of days after the debriefing.'

'Splendid idea. Give me a call as soon as you're ready.'

'I'll do that, Luther. And thanks for the call.'

'Take care of yourself.'

'I will.' And he hung up and cleared the scrambler button.

There was shaving kit and towels on the shelf over the washbasin and he was shaving when Peter Nicholson came in in his dressing gown and slippers.

'What woke you, Tad? I could have slept for a week.'

'I don't know. I think there were some church bells, or maybe I imagined it. And then Luther Meynell phoned.'

'Well it is Sunday, and there's a church up the road a bit. How're you feeling?'

'My mind's still in Moscow but I'll survive.'

'Are you fit enough to talk?'

'Sure. Let's get it over.'

They had breakfast together and Nicholson kept the talk to neutral subjects like pay-scales, promotions and postings, and a problem they'd got at government level in Bonn. After the breakfast things had been cleared away by an orderly Nicholson reached for his briefcase and put it on the table. He opened it, took out a pad and a pen and looked across the table at Anders.

'Have you any objection to having our talk recorded?'

'No. If you think it's necessary.'

'OK. Let's start,' Nicholson paused. 'Where did they pick you up, Tad?'

'In the car.'

'Whereabouts?'

'Just before the underpass. I don't remember the name. I'd need a map.'

'Have you got any idea of how they got on to you?'

'Only theories.'

'Tell me.'

'I think one of Pritchett's men doing the survey was a double agent.'

'He would have known we were interested in Burinski. But he couldn't have known about you or what we intended to do.'

'I think they put a special surveillance on Burinski's flat and on Normannenstrasse. I think they checked on anyone who went near his flat. And I did something stupid that put them on to me.'

'What was that?'

'When I'd checked his flat I checked the square I had

in mind, then I walked along to the office building in Normannenstrasse. There's a taxi stand near there. I took a taxi. The only one that was there. I should have known it was a plant. With their surveillance resources it must have been easy after that.'

'Who interrogated you?'

'A KGB colonel named Kalin.'

'Jesus. Have you seen his file?'

'No. I'd never heard of him.'

'Who beat you up?'

'Two KGB thugs. They didn't introduce themselves.'

'But Kalin gave the order.'

'Yes.'

'He started off as an actor but he did rather nasty things to two or three of his girlfriends and the KGB took him over to save prosecution, and to use his nastier talents.'

'You'd better ask the sixty-four thousand dollar question.'

'What's that?'

Anders shrugged impatiently. 'Did I talk?'

Nicholson looked at Anders' face and then said softly. 'OK. Did you talk?'

'No.'

'How long did they put you through the mincer?'

'Most of it was done on one day. The beating up. They interrogated me off and on for ten days.'

'Then what happened?'

'They started giving me hospital treatment. I suppose the negotiations had started. Then they sent me to a safe-house in the country outside Moscow with Burinski and his wife.'

'Burinski? Is he an interrogator as well?'

'No. He didn't interrogate me, anyway.'

'What happened there?'

'Nothing. I think they were just fattening me up to send back.'

'Why was Burinski's wife there?'

'I think it was just personal. Burinski's very fond of her.'

'She wasn't a KGB swallow trying to lure you into her bed?'

Anders smiled. 'She's six months or maybe seven months pregnant. And she's German.'

'What sort of questions did you get?'

'The usual stuff. Tell uncle all about it first and then when they'd done me over Kalin offered a deal. Answer just one question and Kraus and old Max would go free and I'd only do five years in the Gulag for being a good boy.'

'What was the question?'

'Why Burinski?'

'What did you tell them?'

'Same as before, nothing.'

The telephone rang and Nicholson reached out and picked up the receiver.

'Nicholson . . . yes, he's with me now . . . it's up to you. I'd suggest right now . . . OK.'

When he had hung up he looked at Anders. 'They've sent a quack down from London to check that you're OK. He's here now. I suggested that he got cracking straight away.' Nicholson looked at him. 'Off the record, Tad, how do you feel? Are you all right in yourself?'

'How do I look?'

'Truth or . . .'

'Truth.'

'You look terrible. I'm not sure I would have recognised you in a crowd. If the doctor says things are reasonably under control I suggest you relax for the rest of the day and tomorrow I'll come down and pick you up and you stay with us over the weekend. We'll leave the debriefing for a few days.'

'What day is it today?'

'Thursday.'

'Is it an order that I stay with you?'

'Of course not. I just thought you might like it. I should like it. So would Fleur.'

'OK. Thanks. I'd like to come.'

Fleur Nicholson had a vague idea of what her husband did. It was accepted SIS practice that once a man was as senior as

Nicholson some explanation should, or could, be given to his wife. Wives needed to know why it sometimes happened that their husbands didn't come home that night, to allay their fears until they heard the familiar voice calling from Helsinki, Hong Kong or Washington. A few wives were excluded. Those who were not born British were excluded for their own protection. Those who were promiscuous, tyrants or neurotics were not told for their husband's sake. It was emphasised that their husband's job was responsible and secret and that knowing too much could endanger their husbands and their colleagues. Most wives responded well, but for even the most level-headed there was a period, months or even longer, when they felt as women feel when their homes have been burgled. There had been an intruder and it was hard to decide whether the intruder was SIS or this man who used to be her husband. A strange new man who wasn't any more just a diplomat at the Foreign Office, but a man who lived in a shadowy world where she didn't belong. He was no longer the young man she had met at the tennis-club or a college dance. He had successfully kept it all secret from her, and maybe if he could do that there were other things he could hide from her that were not SIS. For some months he wasn't her husband, and they weren't a pair. Even the fact that he was more important than she had known, more valued by other people, was disturbing.

But Fleur Nicholson, being a Frenchwoman and realistic, had taken it in her stride. If you are attractive and your background was supportive, and if you were raised on the principle that families are parts of dynasties, you have an in-built self-confidence that allows you to see husbands as both *hommes d'affaires* and small boys at the same time. Her husband had told her only that Anders had had a rough time on an assignment and that he was coming for a couple of days rest.

'Is he married yet, Peter?'

'No.'

'Has he got a girlfriend he'd like to bring?'

'I want him to come alone.'

'What about asking your father and mother for Saturday?'
'Good idea if they can make it.'
'Luther Meynell and Patsy?'
'Yes. But keep it small and low-key.'
'Oh, Peter. This stupid jargon. What is low-key, for God's sake? Your father, Luther Meynell – are they low-key?'
Nicholson smiled. 'I mean relaxed and intimate. No climbers, no mixers, no talented queers.'
'You are an idiot. An English idiot.' But she kissed him.

He sat watching them playing tennis. Nicholson and his father, Luther Meynell and his Patsy, Anders wondered how you got to be like them. Taking the big house and its two acres of garden and servants in your stride. It wasn't just a case of money. If he himself were rich he wouldn't live like this. He wouldn't know how to. He didn't know the rules. The Nicholsons were wealthy, but not the Meynells, yet Luther and Patsy Meynell fitted into all this. They belonged. As if belonging was all decided genetically the day you were conceived. He wasn't ill at ease. They seemed to take for granted that he was part of their scene. And they certainly weren't snobs. Maybe Fleur was a bit of a snob, but that was a left-over from the Paris background. A touch of the 16th arrondissement. They talked to their servants as if they were friends, and there was no ostentation. No Bentleys. Not even Jaguars. Rovers for the Nicholsons and a well-cared-for Morris Minor for the Meynells. And yet he wasn't a humble man and on a smaller scale he could have lived this sort of life. So why didn't he?
'Are you warm enough, Tad?'
He looked up. It was Fleur and she was putting up the deckchair beside him.
'I'm fine, thanks. What are the girls doing?'
'Sabine is doing her piano practice, Arlette is counting her pocket-money, and my small namesake is lying on the bed reading a comic instead of tidying her room.' She turned her head to look at him. 'Do you like children, Tad?'

'Yes. But I wouldn't want children of my own.'
'Why not?'
Anders shrugged.
'I'd be scared of not being good for them. Caring too much. Smothering them.'
'My three would love that. Of course it's easier with girls. They like all the loving but they don't inhale all the time.'
He smiled. 'You mean girls are more cynical about loving.'
'They're realistic most of the time. They're a bit like I suspect you are. They lap up the loving but keep in the back of their minds that maybe it's flattery and anyway it won't last for ever.'
'Is that how you see me?'
'Yes. Am I wrong?'
'I've no idea. I don't know what I'm like.'
'You're a nice man, Tad Anders, and that's all that matters. Here's Olga with the drinks, and here come the others.'
It was a calm, restful weekend for Anders. He slept well and the easy-going relationships had taken his thoughts away from Moscow and Berlin. Only when he was alone did he have fleeting visions of the house, the cell, Burinski and Kalin. The atmosphere at the Nicholsons' was almost Victorian. The three pretty young girls were like models from some Pre-Raphaelite painting. He was left to join or leave the family circle and either way he felt at home.

In his room in the house in Tunbridge Wells there were two piles of mail for him. He saw that there were three letters addressed to the PO Box number and seven or eight addressed to him at the club.
He opened the PO Box number letters first. The bulky envelope was a coded statement of payments into his account at a private bank used by SIS and a sheet showing the state of the loan from SIS when he set up the club. The original £8,000 indebtedness was now reduced to £400 and when that was paid, the commentary noted that the lease and small

balance of shares would revert to him. He put it to one side and opened the next letter. He didn't recognise the handwriting on the envelope. The letter was quite brief.

Dear Mr Anders,
I shall be visiting London for a month from the last week in May. I should like to take the opportunity to meet you. I shall be the guest of His Excellency the French Ambassador. Perhaps you would kindly let me know if and when it would be convenient for you.

Yours sincerely,
Julia Crawley (Judy's mother)

Anders read it through a second time before he opened the third envelope. It was a bulky packet. There was no covering note but it contained the documents and the watch that the KGB had taken from him. He knew that it wasn't some burst of generosity or honesty on the part of the men in Dzerdzhinski Square but to let him know that they knew enough about him to be able to use his personal PO Box number.

In the larger pile there was a tart letter from Westminster Council reminding him that he had not reapplied for his permit to operate a private club. Unless . . . etc., etc. There was a letter in green ink from Baldy Morton giving a month's notice. A bill for repairs and garaging of the MGC. A telephone bill for £185.00. There was a long letter from an SIS colleague in Estoril retailing local gossip and wondering if Anders could put him up in June for a seven day leave. A few personal bills. A statement from Barclays of the two club accounts.

Perhaps because the envelope was pink and faintly perfumed he left that letter to the end.

Dearest Tad,
It seems silly to write you at the club when I know you aren't there. But I'm so worried about you. Jacko and Hawks have tried to find out for me what has happened, but there has been no news. I've phoned hospitals and police stations but there was nothing.

I'm so worried about you and I miss you so much. If you ever read this note will you let me know somehow that you're all right. You needn't speak to me if you don't want. Just let me know you're OK.

Your ever loving, (I mean it!!!)
Candy

Anders walked over to the phone and the signal sergeant on the exchange answered.

'Where's Mr Nicholson?'

'I believe he's in Room seven, sir.'

'Can you give me a line.'

'Compliments of Mr Nicholson, sir, can you check with him first?'

Anders hung up and wandered slowly down the landing to Room seven. He knocked on the door and walked in. Nicholson was talking on the telephone but he waved Anders to a seat. When he hung up he turned in his seat.

'You want a call, Tad. Is it urgent?'

Anders passed him Candy's note and sat silently as Nicholson read it. Nicholson looked up smiling and handed it back.

'She's a real sweetie, that kid. Let me contact the club with a message for her. Shall I say you'll be back on Wednesday?'

'That's up to you.'

'We haven't got much more have we?'

Anders shrugged and said nothing.

They had spent another full day going over what had happened. Checking on maps. Filling in descriptions and going over every word he could remember of what had been said to him.

Nicholson had stayed overnight on the Tuesday and had driven him up to London. He had chosen to go on his own to the club.

As he walked through the familiar streets from Leicester Square he felt suddenly happy. Everything was like it always had been. Lively, cheerful and tatty, and he remembered that Burinski's wife had said that Moscow was like someone had switched all the lights off. And for him the lights had just come on again.

As he walked into the club Joey was behind the counter. He looked up, his mouth agape.

'Boss! Mr Anders! We got a message you'd be back tonight, but I didn't believe it. I thought it was a cod. Are you OK?'

'I'm fine, Joey. Did someone pass on a message to Miss Price?'

Joey smiled. 'You bet. She's been in twice. Like a whirling bloody dervish. Half a tick.'

He reached under the counter and brought out a small package and then another. A long tubular something in gift wrapping.

'She brought that in for you. Said she'd be in at seven prompt.'

'What about Baldy? Is he coming in?'

Joey shuffled uncomfortably. 'Yes. He's been in every night. But he don't get on with your friend Mr Travers.'

Anders smiled. 'What happened?'

'Mr Travers tells him what he's got to play. Baldy didn't like that. And he didn't like what he had to play. I don't think the members were too cheerful either.'

'What kind of things?'

'Military marches and rock and roll.'

Anders laughed, picked up his parcels and went to the head of the stairs.

'I'll be in my place, Joey, if there are any calls.'

'Right, sir. Glad to see you back.'

His room looked just as he had left it except for a layer of dust everywhere. Travers obviously hadn't used it. If he had spent his time down in the club it was a wonder that only Baldy had put in his notice. Joe Travers had obviously run a tight ship.

The barman and two of the girls had blitzed through his room with duster and vacuum cleaner and in half an hour it looked reasonably civilised. Somebody had phoned Baldy, and as Anders walked into the club-room he was grinning over the top of the Bechstein as he played a lazy version of 'You were never lovelier'.

When Anders leaned on the lid of the piano Baldy Morton stopped playing.

'Where you been, boss? We all missed you.'

'Missed you too, Baldy.' He pulled a sheet of paper out of his pocket and slid it across the polished lid. It was Baldy Morton's resignation.

'Couldn't read your writing so you'd better keep it.'

The black man grinned and stuffed it into his pocket.

'Just so long as I don't have to play "Ol' man river" again.'

Anders laughed. 'Is that what he wanted?'

'Jesus no. He used to say, "And now one for you, Baldy. Let's have Ol' Man River." He was serious. Trying to be nice.'

Baldy looked past Anders and said quietly, 'Here's Candy. She's been like a ghost since you went away. Real bad, she's been.'

Anders stood up and turned, and she was hurrying through the chairs and tables to him, laughing and crying. And then her arms were round his neck and her wet mouth on his, her hand stroking the back of his neck. She pulled back her head and looked up at him.

'Oh, Tad. I couldn't wait till seven. I had to see you.' Her eyes were on his face. 'You've been ill, haven't you. What was it? You're so thin. Are you really better?'

'I'm fine, sweetie. And it's good to see you. Can you stay?'

'You bet. Did you like your pressies?'

'I've saved them until you came. Let's go up to my place.'

Baldy Morton played 'Love walked in' as they walked away. But nobody listened.

She sat on the settee, watching as he opened the smaller present. It was a digital watch with a built-in calculator. And the note said: 'I worked it out. It's nearly seven million seconds since I saw you.' The tall tube contained a single, long-stemmed red rose and on the heart-shaped card it said,

'I love you so much. Candy.' and there were a lot of scrawled kisses.

The two phones had rung a dozen times before he reached out to the bedside lamp and switched it on. He leaned over her, kissing her gently. And then she frowned and sat up in the bed.

'What on earth are you wearing, Tad?'

And her hand was exploring the bandages round his chest. He pulled her hand gently away.

'It's nothing, sweetie.'

'And you've got a scar with stitch marks on the side of your jaw. Was it a car accident?'

'Something like that. Forget it. Let's go down and say hello to the lads.'

But her eyes were troubled. 'That's not from glass, Tad. It's too neat. That's from a knife, or something sharp.'

'Stop worrying, kid. I'm back, and you're here, and that's all that matters.'

'Can I stay with you tonight?'

'I wish you would. I'd like that.'

Her arms went round him, her head on his shoulder. 'You look ill, Tad. I wish I knew what was the matter.'

'Let's get dressed, honey.'

The club was full, and it was obvious that the word had gone around that the prodigal son was back. Candy's several regular admirers took one look at her happy, smiling face and decided that their propositions would be a waste of time that night. But they were romantic souls and had all sat through TV repeats of *The Sound of Music* at least three times, and knew that love would find a way. And there were, of course, six other pretty girls only too willing to listen to their immodest proposals. There had been champagne toasts from representatives of most criminal activities apart from pushers and ponces. They tended to be foreign and black, and club members were both conservative and prejudiced. Not entirely of course. Jews and Italians rated as true-blue Britishers and shared the same prejudices.

Anders and Candy Price had moved from table to table,

sometimes just standing and chatting for a few minutes, sometimes sitting at a table where Anders knew the people well. Nobody asked where he had been and nobody failed to notice the long livid scar on his jaw. Members frequently went absent from time to time and it would have been reckoned as extremely bad form to enquire where they had been.

It was three o'clock before the club eventually closed, and Anders locked the doors and walked with Candy in the early morning street. Across Leicester Square, along Piccadilly and up Park Lane. Leicester Square still had its complement of riff-raff. Drug-pushers and addicts, pimps and their bedraggled girls, meths drinkers and down-and-outs with their bottles, and the cardboard boxes where they slept until the cleaning machines came round in a couple of hours time. But none of them were aggressive, and Piccadilly itself was almost empty except for a cruising taxi or two, and couples in evening dress strolling back to hotels.

Outside the Hilton and around the Dorchester the parking space was crammed with the Rolls Royces and Cadillacs of oil-rich Arabs, and alongside the Playboy an Arab in full regalia was haggling with a couple of teenage scrubbers as his chauffeur stood by the long-bodied Mercedes with its doors open in invitation.

Just before Marble Arch Anders waved down a taxi and back in Charing Cross Road the sky was beginning to show long fingers of light across Trafalgar Square and down towards the river.

Her mother had sent them a carved, peasant cot with rockers and lace frills, and Burinski sat reading *Pravda*, with one carpet-slippered foot gently rocking the baby as he slept. Inge Burinski was folding nappies and listening to the radio. It was tuned to West Berlin's RIAS and a performance of *The Gypsy Princess*. She had another month before she was due back at the office and Burinski himself seemed to be permanently on the supervision of German-speaking suspects held at Normannenstrasse. For both of them it was the happiest time of their lives. Sergei Vasiliyich Burinski was three months old and as he slept in his rustic cot his parents came as near to praying as their programmed minds would let them, that nothing would disturb their happy world.

Meynell had come down to London by train and taken a taxi to the Travellers. Sir Arthur was a member, and had booked them a private room, and Nicholson was to join them.

The skies were grey outside the big windows and as they waited for Meynell to arrive Nicholson sensed that Sir Arthur's mood matched the weather. He stood gazing into space, not noticing the comings and goings of the waiter who was bringing in the cold meats and bowls of salad so that they could eat and talk undisturbed.

Nicholson was relieved when Meynell was eventually shown up to the room but it seemed to do little to alleviate Sir Arthur's air of gloom. In his preoccupation he was a poor host and Meynell and Nicholson exchanged glances as they passed the plates to each other and French waved them aside. It was almost fifteen minutes after they started eating that Sir Arthur told them what he had planned. And when he finished he avoided looking at either of the others and sat in silence as he waited for a response.

In the beginning Meynell and Nicholson were under the impression that they were being asked to comment on a possible operation in its earliest planning stages. They spoke tentatively and negatively, as one in their doubts about the scheme. But as they chipped away at the logic or lack of logic behind the thinking they slowly came to realise that they had not been invited there to evaluate the plan but to give their approval. Not only was the operation already decided but it was operational. A special team had already been assembled and were undergoing intensive training in Northumberland. And its D-day was only twenty days ahead.

When Meynell, as a totally independent outsider, took the onus of criticism from Nicholson and pointed out how disastrous failure could be, Sir Arthur had almost snarled his rebuttal of the criticisms, and when Nicholson had added his own critical comments and tactfully pointed out the fact that the operation was directly inside his area of responsibility French had turned on him angrily for being 'a wet'.

Eventually, when it was obvious that nothing would change Sir Arthur's mind, they had suggested minor alterations to improve the operation's security and he had accepted them with bad grace. There had been a long and uncomfortable silence before Meynell asked in a quiet voice what he felt would be the repercussions inside SIS if the operation failed. Sir Arthur had thrown his unused table napkin on to the table with a theatrical flourish and said that he would resign.

An official car had been waiting for him and he marked his displeasure by not offering Nicholson a lift. In the taxi back to Century House Nicholson closed his eyes and wondered what lay behind the hare-brained scheme. If it failed, the repercussions would be so widespread that it was impossible to assess them. And if it succeeded the prize was not worth the having.

In his train back to Cambridge Meynell leafed through the pile of magazines that he had bought at the station bookstall. Luther Meynell bought magazines for the same reason that other men bought aspirins or double whiskies. The magazines covered yachting, photography, hi-fi and model trains. And the current issue of *Encounter* for reading in bed. Despite his carefully contrived diversions his mind did go back for fleeting moments to the room in the Travellers and French's grim face and grimmer news. But Meynell was older than Nicholson. In one area of life or another he had seen it all before. It was all too often desk-bound men who planned the bloodiest operations. War salved their consciences but in peacetime they paid with neuroses, and if they indulged their frustrations too often the price was psychoses.

Unlike some of his associates Meynell had considerable respect for French's brain. It had been sharp and penetrating in the old days and he had had a sense of humour in those days too. Admittedly it was a mordant humour that made more enemies than friends, but it was usually the truth even if it was always so cruelly barbed. It was probably that wretched ex-wife of his who had done the damage. Thank God it had been short and sharp, not one of those long drawn out wars of attrition that bright minds so often indulged in. Maybe the security organisations should look more carefully at a man's private life. Undemocratic, uncivilised, it might be, but at certain levels many men's lives could depend on one man's state of mind. And at other levels years of painstaking diplomacy could be made worthless by the latest outburst of some virago. They checked for homosexuality, gambling, promiscuity and drinking, but they were rare enough or common enough in all men, to be at least visible and capable of being monitored. But how did you monitor the canker in a man's heart or a festering wound in his psyche? French thought that he was taking positive action but he wasn't. It was merely extravagant reaction, and in the Intelligence services more disasters flowed from precipitate reaction than any other cause.

Meynell sighed and turned back to his magazines and picked out the *New Statesman* and *Spectator*. He wondered why he bought the NS any longer. Except for Arthur Marshall and Roger Woddis it was virtually unreadable. Just nostalgia, and a trip down Memory Lane.

Chapter 13

He sat waiting in the residents' lounge at the Connaught for half an hour and he had no doubt that the waiting was intentional. When the meeting had been arranged on the telephone she had told him how to get to the Connaught as if he was unlikely to know where it was.

Then one of the under-managers came up to him. 'Mr Anders?'

'Yes.'

He turned and looked towards a slim blonde woman standing at the entrance to the lounge.

'Mrs Crawley to see you, sir.'

Anders stood up and walked over to the woman. She had sad, haunted eyes and a forced social smile. She moved her handbag from one arm to the other to avoid shaking hands.

'Well, Mr Anders, we meet at last.'

'Would you like a drink or shall we go straight in and have lunch?'

'It's very kind of you but I have a lunch appointment. A drink, perhaps.'

Anders followed her to a table and two chairs in the furthest corner of the room. She asked for a Bloody Mary and he settled for a tomato juice. When he turned to look at her she was already looking at him.

'It was good of you to meet me, Mr Anders.' She paused. 'I'm sure you know that what I have to say will not be agreeable to you.'

Anders looked back at her without comment. A nerve quivered on her cheek and he realised that under the veneer of self-confidence she was, in fact, tense and nervous.

'Judy's very fond of you, I know that. And I know you love her, but it can't go on, Mr Anders. It really can't. She's a very young girl and she's not capable of coping with this sort of situation. She's utterly confused, you know. We've had long talks with her, my husband and I, and we've made quite clear where her duty and her future lie. She must go back to her husband.'

She waited while the glasses were put on the table and when they were alone she turned to look at him again. She managed a weak, mouth-trembling smile. She had said her piece. The worst was over.

'Why did he send you, Mrs Crawley? Why didn't he come himself?'

'He's very busy. Committees and so on. I'm sure you understand.'

'I understand all right, Mrs Crawley. I know from what I've heard that he's a bully, and bullies are always cowards. I'm sorry that you've had to do his dirty work for him. But if Judy agreed with you both, and your advice, you wouldn't be here. So what's the problem?'

She looked away for a moment and there were tears at the edges of her eyes. Then she turned back to look at him.

'You're a very attractive man, Mr Anders. I can understand why Judy wants to run off with you. I really can. But her father would never forgive her. She would be completely cut off from her family. She wouldn't like that, Mr Anders, I assure you.'

'Nobody would, Mrs Crawley. But she's twenty-nine and old enough to decide her own life. My impression is that she doesn't want to go back to her husband. And for the record she didn't run off with me. As you well know she had left her husband long before she even met me.'

'She would go back to him if you were not an alternative. Maybe not for love, but out of duty to us all.'

'So?'

'So we ask that you don't see her again.'

'What do you think that will do for her? To be rejected by someone she relies on.'

She shook her head slowly. 'I don't know, Mr Anders. I really don't know.' She turned her head to look at him, her hand on his arm. 'She would get over it. I know from my own experience. In the end the pain goes and we just live our lives.'

'I haven't seen Judy for over three months. I've been away for some time and I haven't contacted her since I came back. Perhaps she has already made up her mind to go along with your advice.'

She half-smiled. 'You know that isn't true, Mr Anders. Or I should not be here. She has tried to contact you several times but the man said you were away for a long time. If she knew you were back she would contact you.'

'We'd better wait and see if she does.'

'That means you won't cooperate, Mr Anders?'

'No. I won't cooperate.'

She stood up. 'I'd better go. I've done my best.'

He heard the echo of rehearsal in her words. That was what she would say to her husband.

'I'll walk to the door with you and get you a taxi.'

There was no need. There were two taxis waiting and as he opened the door for her she turned and looked at him. She said softly, 'I wish I could run away with you, too.' And she kissed him on the cheek.

It was almost two weeks later that Judy called him. She sounded cheerful enough, almost perky. She didn't ask where he had been or how he was. But she wanted to see him as soon as possible. When he suggested that she came round right away it seemed that it wasn't that urgent. It was Tuesday and could he make it the Thursday evening of the next week? He agreed, and speaking in almost a whisper she told him she loved him, and he said he loved her too.

It was only an hour later that he got the call from Peter Nicholson. They wanted him at a meeting urgently. A private room had been booked at the Hilton; could he be there in half an hour? He said he would be there.

It was raining very slightly as he got out of the taxi and walked towards the big glass doors. A security man at a small table near the entrance checked him perfunctorily and then he walked across the foyer to the lifts. The room number that Nicholson had given him was a suite on the fifth floor and it was Meynell who opened the door when he knocked.

'Come in, Tad. We're all here. A whisky?'

'A malt if you've got one. Neat.'

'Glenlivet or Glen Grant?'

'Glen Grant.'

Sir Arthur French and Nicholson already had drinks and as Anders took the glass it was French who set the ball rolling. Anders thought that he must have been on holiday. His eyes were bright and the pallor had gone from his cheeks. He looked alert and in control. He smiled a tight smile towards Anders who was conscious of the other two watching him intently.

'We've squared the account for you, Tad.'

'What account is that, Sir Arthur?'

'The account with the KGB.'

'I don't understand.'

'We've got Burinski.'

There was a long silence and then Anders said softly, 'How do you mean, you've *got* him?'

'We sent a team in. Picked him up and got him out.'

'When was this?'

'Five days ago. It all went very smoothly.'

'Well . . . congratulations.'

French caught the hesitation and knew that the others would have caught it too. It riled him, but the euphoria from the success of the operation was still pumping the adrenalin into his system when he talked or thought about it.

'We want you to do the interrogation. A thorough debriefing.'

'But after five days, surely you're well into it by now?'

'He's not been well, Tad. We had to get a doctor to him.'

'You mean he was beaten up?'

'Of course not. He's . . . well . . .' he turned to Nicholson who took the hint.

'He just folded, Tad. Shit-scared and shocked. Nobody's laid a finger on him.'

Anders looked from one to the other in disbelief. 'Why was this done?'

Sir Arthur didn't hesitate. 'When your operation failed it didn't remove the original reasons for wanting Burinski. We want to know what the *Spetsburo* are doing and if they're spreading their remit beyond West Germany. We need to know who the staff are and what the general set-up consists of.'

'I see.' Anders sounded unconvinced as he leaned back in his chair.

Meynell took up the threads. 'He's asked a number of times to see you, Tad. We think he'd talk if you got alongside him.'

'You obviously made an impression on him.' French made it sound as if it were a fault on Anders' part rather than a virtue.

Anders looked at Meynell. 'I'm not a trained interrogator, Luther. It's not my line at all.'

'That doesn't matter. We can have a brief prepared for you to start with and you can be briefed each day after you've done your report. You will just be talking to him. It won't be a formal interrogation. When we see how it's going we'll tell you the areas we want you to explore.'

'Where is he?'

'At the safe-house in Ebury Street,' Nicholson said.

'I'd like to talk to him before I decide.'

'Decide what?' French's voice was sharp.

'Decide whether I want to do it or not.'

'It's an official request, Mr Anders.' French's cheeks were flushed with anger and he leaned forward aggressively. Anders looked back at him.

'So get somebody official to do it, Sir Arthur.'

There were several seconds of silence. Both Nicholson and Meynell would have admitted to themselves that they fleetingly enjoyed Sir Arthur's dilemma but Meynell was too mature to let him flounder even though he deserved it.

'I spoke to Burinski myself. Very briefly. He's very worried about his wife and child and I gathered from what he said that you spent quite a time with her and Burinski. He's certainly got great respect for you, and I think he'd talk to you, Tad. I'd guess he's a bit of a hero-worshipper.'

Anders nodded. 'Maybe. But that's why I want to talk to him before I decide.'

'What doubts have you got about doing it?'

Anders shrugged. 'I don't really know. It isn't a standard relationship.'

Meynell smiled. 'What's worrying you? The Judas factor?'

Anders smiled back. 'Maybe. I just don't know.'

Meynell turned to French. 'Why doesn't Peter take Tad over to see our friend and then we could talk again.'

Sir Arthur obviously resented someone else offering a solution, but it was a solution all the same, and he turned to Nicholson.

'Is that OK with you, Peter?'

'Yes.' Nicholson stood up, aware that French wasn't going to have the courtesy to ask if it was convenient for Anders. 'It won't take long, Tad.'

As they went down in the lift to the Hilton's underground carpark Nicholson said, 'Don't take any notice of French, Tad. Meynell and I were very much against this operation. We thought it would end up as a total disaster. French had got the bit between his teeth so we had no choice. And give him his due it went off exactly to plan. Mind you, it had a cast like Ben-Hur. And we do need to know a hell of a lot more about the *Spetsburo* and what it's up to. We didn't take too much interest when it seemed to be confined to West Germany but now they've started over here we've got to clobber them right at the start.'

'Who was it suggested a trade for me? I bet it wasn't Sir Arthur.'

'It was Luther Meynell, but French went along with it without any great pressure.'

'Why did they abandon the rules?'

'Guilt. They knew they'd not bothered enough. When it was evaluated, Stoppard's report was blistering. Tore it to pieces. Suggested an enquiry to see if undue pressure had been put on you that could explain why you agreed to go.' He smiled without looking at Anders. 'They're bastards, I know. But not total bastards.'

Burinski was lying on the bed fully clothed. Nicholson left Anders to go in on his own. Anders walked over to the bed, pulled over one of the chairs and sat down.

'You wanted to see me, Vasili.'

The Russian turned his head to look at Anders' face. He looked for several minutes without speaking and then he said, 'I know from your face that you won't help me.'

'What help do you want?'

'I want to go back. I want to be released.'

'You must know that that isn't possible.'

'Why not?'

'You came over here and committed a political murder. You're KGB, and you're a trained assassin.'

'The man was a Jugoslav. He wasn't British.'

'Makes no difference. You know that.'

'You know what will happen to Inge and my child.'

'Tell me.'

'The child will be put in a State orphanage and Inge will be sent to a labour camp.'

'Why should they do that?'

'You know how it works, comrade. You know as well as I do.'

'Maybe they'll offer an exchange for you.'

'Never. Not for a *Spetsburo* man. They don't admit that the *Spetsburo* exists.'

'So what do you want me to do?'

Burinski sat up and swung his legs down to the floor, leaning forward to look at Anders.

'How if I talk with you, answer all your questions? Everything you want to know?'

'Go on.'

'You get my wife and son out, and you let us all live here. I could work for SIS.'

'Is that what you want?'

Burinski shrugged. 'There is nothing else.'

'They will probably say that they will only consider it after you've talked.'

'Then I don't talk.'

'You'll talk in the end, Vasili. People always do.'

'You didn't talk.'

Anders smiled. 'Kalin is an oaf. Beating up professionals doesn't make them talk, it makes them all the more determined not to cooperate. But people always do talk sooner or later. There are other ways than physical violence.'

'Would they have made you talk?'

'Who knows? Maybe in the end. It's possible.'

'So you won't help me?'

'I didn't say that. I told you what the official view might be. That you talk first, and then maybe something could be worked out depending on how cooperative you were.'

Burinski shook his head. 'No. First we make a bargain. Then I will talk.'

'I'll tell them what you've said.'

'You understand, don't you?'

'I understand both sides, Vasili. That's why I'm sure they won't agree.'

'Maybe you can negotiate some compromise for me.'

'Maybe. I'll think about it.'

And then quite suddenly Burinski was sobbing, his hands to his face, his body shivering as if he had an ague. For a few seconds Anders sat there, surprised by the outburst, and then he put his hand on the Russian's bowed shoulder, waiting for the sobs to die away.

He turned as he heard the door open. It was Nicholson, and Anders waved him away. It was a long time before Burinski's sobs died down and he lifted his head, his eyes closed and his face wet with his tears.

'What is it, Vasili?'

'I might just as well have killed them with my own hands. Both of them.' He was shaking his head as he stared at

Anders. 'They don't deserve it. They have done nothing. Nothing at all.'

Anders said quietly. 'It's what happens to hundreds of people every day in the Soviet Union. You know that, Vasili. You're part of the system.'

'She had no idea what I did. She knew I was KGB but that was all. She'll die in a labour camp. What can I do? Tell me.'

'I'll talk to my people and see what they say.'

'You'll try very hard?'

'Of course.'

'She liked you so much. She was so impressed that you warned her not to talk in that place. She said you were a very special man.'

The tears were falling again and Anders put his hand on Burinski's knee.

'Have some sleep and I'll see what I can do.'

Burinski nodded, swallowing his tears, unable to speak.

They had been away just over an hour, and Meynell and French were still talking in the suite. They fell silent as Anders sat down.

'He's in a state about his wife and child. Afraid that she'll be sent to the Gulag and the child to an orphanage.'

Sir Arthur shrugged. 'He's probably right.'

'He says that he'll talk with me, answer any questions we ask, provided he can stay here and we get his wife and child out.'

Sir Arthur smiled. 'And if we don't?'

'He says he won't talk at all.'

Meynell stood up. 'D'you think he means it, Tad?'

'I think he meant it but I'd guess that he'll talk in the end. He's not trained as an agent. He's an assassin and nothing more. His victims were unarmed and taken by surprise. You don't need all that much guts to do that. Just a programmed mind. But if he didn't talk voluntarily I'd say it would be a very slow process.'

'How long, Tad?'

'Months. Six or seven. Isolation treatment, and the rest of it. He'd hope that his not talking would filter back to Moscow and might help his wife.'

French leaned back in his chair. 'Well there's no question of getting the wife and child out. They're probably not there now. And if she were I wouldn't authorise it.'

Anders stood up. 'Peter can tell him tomorrow, then. I'd say he needs a psychiatrist right now or he'll be in a hopeless state in a few days.'

As Anders turned to leave French said, 'Mr Anders.'

Anders turned and looked at him. 'Yes?'

'Sit down. Mr Anders, I haven't finished.'

'I have, Sir Arthur. Let someone else deal with him.'

'Tad. Sit down please.' Meynell was looking at him with a quizzical look, his head on one side. 'Let's be sensible, Tad. Let's talk it out.'

Anders sighed, walked back to the chair and sat down.

Meynell said, 'He *is* willing to talk with you?'

'Yes.'

'Everything? Not just answer questions?'

'Yes, he'll cooperate fully.'

'But only if we get out his wife and child?'

'So he says.'

'You think he means it?'

'Yes. He's very dependent on his wife. He loves her. It's as simple as that. He thinks of it as if he had killed them himself.'

'And if we don't do the deal, you think he will talk but it may take months?'

'Yes.'

Meynell looked across at Sir Arthur. 'How urgent is this, Arthur?'

'For heaven's sake, Luther, I got the Minister's agreement to mount this operation because we need to know about the *Spetsburo*. Bonn has been raising hell for months, threatening to go it alone. We need to show results right now.'

"*Could* we get them out?'

'If they're in Berlin it's possible. But they'll be under

constant surveillance. They may take them to Moscow. Even in Berlin it would be well nigh impossible without losing lives.'

'We ran that risk to get *him* out.'

Sir Arthur looked up sharply. '*I* ran the risk, Luther. And I ran the risk despite your and Nicholson's wet-blanket attitude because I thought it was necessary. I don't feel this is necessary. Who the hell is this . . . this criminal, to lay down conditions?'

Meynell said softly, 'He's the man who can tell us what we want to know. He's the man who can make your operation a total success.'

Sir Arthur gestured impatiently. 'For God's sake don't butter me up, Luther. I'm too old for that.'

Meynell turned to the other two. 'I wonder if you two would care to leave us for a bit. Say half an hour.'

Anders and Nicholson strolled down to the first floor and ordered a drink. As they sat in the lounge the pianist was playing 'Some Enchanted Evening' but you could barely hear it for the noise. It was louder and shriller than at the club.

They lingered a little longer than the half hour and then walked back up instead of taking the lift. Meynell looked cheerful as he let them in, and after they had sat down French said his piece.

'Luther and I have gone over this wretched situation a dozen times. He's convinced me that we should go along with Burinski's demands. But with one condition.' He wagged a monitory finger at Anders. 'You tell him we will use our best endeavours to get his wife and child out, but there's no guarantee. Is that understood?'

Anders shrugged. 'I'll put it to him and see what he says.'

Sir Arthur opened his mouth to speak and then changed his mind.

Meynell said quickly, 'Why not go back on your way to the club and put him out of his misery?'

Nicholson said, 'I'll drive you, Tad, and then take you on to your place.'

Anders sat without speaking as Nicholson drove him back to Ebury Street. As he got out he looked at his watch and could hardly believe it was only eight-thirty.

Burinski's face was white and drawn as he saw Anders come into the room.

'I've talked to them, Vasili. Provided you cooperate fully, they will agree to what you want. But we want everything you know. Names, backgrounds, organisation, everything. You understand?'

He thought for a moment that Burinski was going to faint and then the Russian said, 'My God. My God. I thank you with all my heart. I really do. I'll cooperate any way you want.'

'It will take time to get them out, Vasili. They will be under twenty-four hour surveillance for some time.'

'I understand, comrade. We are professionals, you and I. Your people's word is all I ask.'

'Get some sleep and I'll see you in a couple of days.'

'I'll start making notes right away, and . . . what can I say? I can rest again.'

Nicholson drove Anders to Leicester Square and he walked on his own to the club. He was probably the only man in the world for whom the stretch from Piccadilly Circus to Charing Cross Road was home.

Back at the club he bathed and shaved and changed into shirt and slacks. As he poured himself a whisky he pressed his hand against the pain in his chest. Seeing Burinski had brought all those black thoughts back again. The bastards had thrown him to the wolves unprotected, but when they wanted something it was suddenly possible to mount a full-scale operation. Time and expense no object. But they *had* traded for him. He had to give them that. Why had he joined them and not made it clear to Burinski that if they couldn't get her and the child out he'd have wasted his breath? But that sort of thinking was crazy. The bastard was a KGB man who specialised in political murder. Burinski would spend no time worrying about other people's wives and children. And Burinski himself would be alive and free, and that was a hell of a lot more than he could expect. Then the pain stabbed at the back of his head. He reached for the bottle of pills that the SIS doctor had given him after the check-up. He'd said that he'd have pain for another six months but the attacks would gradually be more spaced out. If they got unbearable despite the pills he'd have to go in and they would do an exploratory operation. He took the two pills with a sip of whisky and then he slowly stood up and stretched his arms. Ignore it and it would go away.

The club was half empty that night and they closed just after midnight. He sat with Candy looking at a late film on TV and they were in bed before one.

When he heard the shouting he jumped out of bed and staggered to the window. But he couldn't find the window and then a light went on and he shielded his eyes. There was sweat pouring down his body but he was cold and shivering as he reached out to steady himself. And there was a naked girl saying something a long way away. As his eyes focused he saw that it was Candy but his eyes still searched for the window. There was no window. He was in his bedroom and it didn't have a window. And the shouting had died away.

'Tad. What's the matter, love? What is it. Come and lie down.'

She led him to the bed and as he sat there she pulled the duvet round his shoulders.

'Shall I phone for a doctor, Tad?'

'It woke me up, the shouting.'

'It was you, Tad. You were talking and shouting.'

He turned his head slowly to look at her. 'What was I on about?'

'I don't know. You weren't speaking English. I couldn't understand. You sounded afraid.'

'I'm OK, sweetie. It must have been a nightmare.'

'You're poorly, Tad. You need a doctor.'

He looked at her pretty face, her big eyes were frightened but full of concern as they looked back at him.

'You know something, kid?'

'No. What?'

'I love you, Candy Price. I certainly do.'

He lay back on the bed and as she covered him up she knew that whatever it was it had passed. His big, deep chest was rising and falling evenly, and he was already asleep.

She let him sleep until ten. The outside phone with the little box beside it rang several times but she didn't answer it.

When she woke him he seemed quite normal but he didn't talk much as he sat drinking the black coffee. As he put the cup and saucer on to the bedside table he turned to look at her.

'What day is it today?'

'Thursday.'

'Are you doing anything special the next few days?'

She smiled. 'I never do anything special, Tad, you know that.'

'How about we go away for a few days. Somewhere quiet.'

'Both of us?'

'Of course.'

'Oh, I'd love that. Where shall we go?'

He smiled. 'It's a surprise.'

'Your phone has rung two or three times.'

He looked alarmed. 'You didn't answer it?'

'Of course not.'

'Good girl. D'you need to get clothes or anything?'

'Of course I do.'

'How long will it take?'

'If I go now I could be back by twelve.'

'OK. You do that.'

Anders put down the hood of the white MGC and they both felt relaxed as they headed down the A21 as far as the turning to Battle where they stopped for lunch. It was mid-afternoon when Anders pulled up outside the cottage in the narrow lane, to open the two gates to the short driveway. When he had parked the car he got their bags out of the boot.

Candy was standing by the car looking at the cottage and when Anders joined her she said, 'Who does it belong to, Tad?'

'Me.'

She turned to look at his face. 'How long have you had it?'

'Six, seven years, I don't remember exactly.'

'Who knows about it?'

'Nobody. Just you and me.'

'It's beautiful, Tad. And it's so quiet here.'

'Let's go in and make ourselves at home. It'll be a bit dusty.'

The cottage was built of local stone with a thatched roof over two dormer windows. On the ground floor there were two small windows set in the whitewashed wall and the door was solid oak with old-fashioned wrought-iron fittings. Inside there was one medium-sized living room with heavy oak beams and alongside was a small modern kitchen and a bathroom. A narrow staircase led to the two bedrooms upstairs.

From the front the cottage was half-hidden from the lane by a weeping willow on the long narrow lawn. At the back was a sloping lawn with a dozen or so fruit trees; and a white post and rail fence marked off the boundaries from the fields that sloped gradually down to the valley.

Immediately outside the kitchen door was an area of bricks in herring-bone fashion and an old oak bench against the wall. They sat there drinking tea from china mugs, the girl's hand resting on Anders' thigh.

'It's so beautiful, Tad. It's like a cottage from a fairy story.'

'Is it too quiet for you? Too isolated?'

'Of course not. That's what makes it so good.'

'We've got four days, sweetie, before we have to go back.'

'Why didn't you ever tell anyone about it?'

'I didn't want anyone to know about it.'

'And nobody's ever been here before?'

'No. Just me.'

'How often do you come here?'

'Not often. Four or five times a year.'

'What do you do?'

'Nothing much. Read, sleep, eat and think.'

She put her hand up to his cheek and turned his head to look at her. 'Why did you ask me to come with you?'

'I just like being with you.'

'Why?'

He sighed. 'Because you're pretty, because I like making love to you, and because you care about me.'

'I do care about you, Tad. So much.'

'I care about you too, kid. But I'm old enough to be your father.'

'Why should that matter, for God's sake?'

'It doesn't. I don't know why I said it.'

'I do.'

'Why?'

'Because something happened to you while you were away. And you're depressed, and you *should* see a doctor. You're very low, Tad, and you shouldn't be.'

'Why not?'

'Tad, love, you own the club, you make a good living, everybody likes you. You're a special kind of man and you always will be. You'll be fine again when you've had a few days rest.'

Anders stood up. 'Let's go and look at the sea.'

She smiled. 'I'll have to buy you a bucket and spade.'

They ate at small country inns and small cafés on the coast, they made love and slept for long peaceful hours, and as the girl had predicted, Anders recovered his equilibrium. They sat in the sun on their last morning, on the bench outside the kitchen door, Candy reading a Mills and Boon romance and Anders sitting watching her as she turned the pages slowly, intent on the story.

'Candy.'

She put the book on her lap and turned, smiling, to look at him.

'What is it, Tad?'

'Will you marry me, Candy?'

Her smile faded and she looked at him, surprise and disbelief on her face.

'You don't mean that, Tad.'

'I do.'

'Why me?' she said softly.

'Because you care about me, and I care about you.'

She sat looking at his face for a long time. 'Sometimes I wish you weren't such an honest man.'

'Why?'

'I'll tell you some day.'

'You haven't answered me.'

She shook her head. 'What about Judy?'

'What about her?'

'You care about her too.'

'She doesn't care about me. I think she'll go back to her husband sooner or later.'

'Did you ever ask her to marry you?'

He sighed, 'Yes.'

'What did she say?'

'She said yes.'

'But never quite got around to doing anything about it. Like getting a divorce for instance.'

He half-smiled but didn't reply. She saw the dullness come back into his eyes and said quickly, 'So let me be truthful, Tad Anders, just like you are. I'd do anything to be married to you. Absolutely anything. But I happen to love you. Really love you. So I'd want to be sure that I'd make you happy. I'd willingly marry you tomorrow even if I thought that I was going to be unhappy every day of my life, but I wouldn't want that for you. I'd like to walk round Soho right now, shouting out – "Tad Anders has asked me to marry him. The wedding's next Saturday". But I want to be sure, my love, that it's going to be right for you.'

'So?'

'So I'll give you my answer in a few weeks. I desperately want it to be yes. At the worst it'll be "let's wait a bit longer".'

'What do you want to do now?'

She smiled and kissed him on the mouth. 'I'll give you one guess.'

He smiled, stood up, and took her hand.

'Did you ever meet Sudoplatov?'

'I attended lectures by him but I never talked with him as an individual.'

'When did he take over the *Spetsburo*?'

'During the war he was in charge of the Fourth Directorate of the NKVD and when the *Spetsburo* was set up he was in charge from the start.'

'When was that?'

'In 1946.'

'Where does it operate?'

'Mainly Germany, Austria and Switzerland but it's allowed to operate anywhere.'

'Are only Soviets recruited?'

'All supervision is by Soviets but a lot of East Germans and Czechs are recruited for physical violence.'

'How are they recruited?'

'They're almost all criminals and they're recruited from the prisons.'

'What was the Fourth Directorate responsible for in the war?'

'They trained and operated the partisans for espionage and assassination behind the German lines.'

Anders looked at the notes on his clipboard, holding the pause button on the tape-recorder.

'According to our records the *Spetsburo* was disbanded in June 1953. Is that incorrect?'

'Students were not told about that but it was well-known that it was disbanded. It was only for a few months, because Khrushchev decided that he needed it. It became the 9th section of the First Chief Directorate, and when the KGB was founded in 1954 the *Spetsburo* became Department 13 of the First Chief Directorate.'

'Tell me about Kalin. How long has he been *Spetsburo*?'

'He isn't *Spetsburo*. He's 2nd Department of second Chief Directorate. He's a deputy on the British Commonwealth desk.'

'Did you know in advance that I was going to pick you up?'

'Others did. I wasn't told beforehand.'

'How did they know about me?'

'We were using a double-agent. He was told to do surveillance on me by one of your people and he kept the KGB informed. They weren't sure who you were or what you were going to do but they cleared all the taxi stands around the area. You took a taxi that was KGB and you were under surveillance all the time after that.'

'Let's go back to your training period.'

'Can I have a rest, comrade? I find it hard work trying to remember all these details.'

'OK. I'll raise some tea for you.'

Anders took the tape-recorder and the technical sergeant took off the spool and laced up a clean one. The used spool covered fourteen hours of interrogation.

Tape spools were analysed during the night. Sliced into half hour segments they were listened to by a team, and by the following morning a new list of questions or re-checks was ready for Anders. There were few re-checks because it wasn't an interrogation, it was a voluntary debriefing. But despite Burinski's cooperation discrepancies arose and had to be checked because SIS's information on the *Spetsburo* was sparse and the CIA were to be offered the transcript in exchange for their information on both the *Spetsburo* and the *Kamera*.

Anders and Burinski kept at it day after day, four or five hours a day.

It sometimes happens that an interrogating officer who carries out a long interrogation with a subject gradually comes to identify with the man. Their recruitment, training and work was often almost identical. But Anders felt no such identification with Burinski. As a man he despised him, and the total ruthlessness of the *Spetsburo* and its controllers aroused the anti-Soviet, and anti-Russian feelings that most

Poles felt for the country that had ravaged Poland so many times in its history.

SIS was ruthless when it needed to be, and Anders was one of its operators, but the *Spetsburo* wasn't the same. SIS operated against the foreign enemies of Britain, but the *Spetsburo* killed and tortured for political reasons just to keep the thugs of the Politburo in power. But Anders was shrewd enough, and professional enough, to keep his distaste for the man well hidden. The West Germans had been placated by the operation that lifted Burinski and had asked for the opportunity of interrogating him themselves, but so far their request had been diplomatically fobbed off, at least until Anders had finished.

Chapter 14

LUTHER MEYNELL sat in the corner seat of the carriage looking out over the flat East Anglican landscape. And as he looked at the peaceful countryside he tried to assemble a rational argument. But there *was* no rational argument. When he and French had talked together that evening at the Hilton they had both known what they were doing. They had never said it out loud even to each other, but they knew it all the same. All that had mattered was getting the Russian to talk. If he didn't, then huge resources in time and money had been wasted. And what also mattered was that they needed the information to head off the West Germans from going it alone. Going it alone would have given Moscow just the excuse it was looking for to try and take over the whole of Berlin. Maybe they wouldn't have done it, but with that sort of provocation they'd have gone on the rampage somewhere. And the Russian would only talk if they agreed to his totally unreasonable demands.

Meynell reached for his copy of *The Times* and opened it, turning to the letters page. Then with a sigh he folded the paper and tossed it on to the empty seat opposite. All that rationalising was a lot of hogwash. Both he and French had known that there was no question of getting out the woman and the child. Even if the man had come over voluntarily as a defector it wouldn't have been on. And to mount an operation on that scale for such a purpose would have been preposterous. To do it for an assassin who had been picked up and brought over by their own people was out of the question.

Both he and French had been sure that the wife and child would have been moved to Moscow, and nobody would know better than Burinski himself that they would be crazy to try and get her out. And they could have emphasised the risk to the woman's life and the dire punishment she and the child would suffer if the operation went wrong. But she hadn't been removed to Moscow, she was still there with the child in East Berlin. The evaluation team had even put up the theory that the KGB had left them in East Berlin as a bait, and a check on whether Burinski had talked or not. They could have decided that if he talked he may try to make a bargain with SIS about getting them out, and if an attempt was made the trap would close and then there would be yet another set of problems.

But none of it, the rationalising, the actual facts, could hide the fact that Burinski had talked and they had no intention of lifting a finger to get out his wife and child. What nobody would know, or at least what nobody could prove, was the fact that both he and French had known this when Anders and Nicholson came back that night. Neither he nor French had said it out loud. But both of them had known what was in the other's mind.

Nicholson wouldn't like it, but he would accept the facts of life and console himself that he had been no part of the deception. He had no idea of how Anders would take it. Anders would feel differently because he knew the wife. He had a relationship with both of them. He would probably feel that he had been deceived or exploited. And then that Slav temperament could explode in all directions. On the other hand Burinski had watched the KGB thugs beat up Anders. *He* hadn't offered Anders any helping hand. Anders wouldn't have forgotten that. He could be reminded of it too. Maybe he would take it all in his stride. He doubted it, but it was to give it that chance that French had asked *him* to tell Anders. And Meynell had wrung out of French an assurance that there would be no come-back on Anders. Now that SIS had all the *Spetsburo* information that Burinski could give, French wanted the whole affair forgotten. Burinski wouldn't be tried, he would merely be a prisoner in that grim, silent house on the west coast of Scotland. He's be there until he died. And as far as Sir Arthur was concerned he could be dead already.

He just wanted it all over and done with. Burinski out of the way, the information in the files, and Anders appeased.

At Liverpool Street Meynell walked slowly towards the taxi rank. He looked up at the glassed-in roof but it was too grimy to give any indication of the weather outside. He had slept fitfully for the last half hour of the journey but his mind felt duller rather than brighter. He wondered for a moment why people started campaigns to preserve monstrosities like this station. It was probably because they never used the damn place themselves.

The taxi dropped him at the corner of Great Newport Street and he walked the rest of the way to the club. The doors were open and there was a bucket and vacuum cleaner in the middle of the floor. He reached over to the counter and pressed the bell marked 'Press', and waited. He looked around at the walls with their blistered brown paint, the primitive row of hangers for coats, and an umbrella propped on a saucer in the far corner of the room. It was hard to connect Anders and SIS, and Berlin and Moscow, with this incongruous place. He pressed the bell again and looked at the centrefolds stacked up on the wall behind the counter. They were curling at the bottom edges but the young girls were really beautiful. He wondered if the photographer had sex with the models afterwards. And then a young man wearing an old blue anorak came in from the street.

'You waiting to join, mister? There's a waiting list at the moment nearly . . .'

'Will you tell Mr Anders that his visitor has arrived, please?'

'What name shall I give?'

'Just be kind enough to give him that message.'

The youth picked up one of the phones and pressed one of the square buttons.

'Your visitor's here, boss.'

He listened then put down the phone and looked at Meynell.

'He says to go right up, sir. He's waiting for you.'

Meynell nodded and made his way carefully down the

main stairs and then along the corridor that reeked of Lysol and urine and an obnoxious smelling air-freshener.

Anders was waiting for him at the top of the far set of stairs.

Inside the room Anders turned to his visitor.

'A sherry, Luther?'

'I'll have a whisky if I may.'

When they were both sitting Anders said, 'Peter Nicholson said you were down for some academic meeting.'

Meynell shook his head, 'I wish I was. I'm down here to talk with you.'

He saw Anders' eyes narrow like a dog expecting a blow and hated even more what he was about to do. Anders had grown to expect anything from SIS to be unpleasant. Meynell shifted in his chair and drew a deep breath.

'I've got something unpleasant to say, Tad. I've no idea what your reaction will be except that I don't expect you'll like it. All I ask is that you'll think about it as unemotionally as you can before you reach your conclusions.'

'Sounds pretty grim, Luther, you'd better tell me what it is.'

'There's no chance of getting out Burinski's wife and child.'

There was a long silence as they looked at each other.

'Where is she?'

'Still at their flat in East Berlin.'

'So what's the problem?'

Meynell sighed. 'Two problems. We've had an evaluation team report that suggests that she's being left there to see if we try and get her out. If we do, they'll know that we're doing it because Burinski has talked. It's taken for granted that the flat is under continuous surveillance and that any attempt to get them out would fail. Disastrously.'

'You said there were two problems. What's the other?'

'There was never any intention to get them out. We just wanted Burinski to talk.'

Anders poured himself another drink before he looked back at Meynell.

'So you and French lied to me. Deliberately.'

'I'm afraid so, Tad. We didn't discuss it or agree to lie. I think we just both separately knew that it wasn't on, but we needed Burinski's information. And we didn't *promise* to do it.'

'You said we would do our best.'

'I know. I said that myself. It was a lie, and I knew it was a lie. I had a vague hope that things might turn out so that it wasn't a lie but I knew in my mind that it was a vain hope. You must blame me, not French.'

'Why not French?'

'I said the words. He didn't.'

'You were speaking for the two of you. He didn't contradict you.'

'I think maybe he would have told you right out that he wouldn't authorise it. I spoke up because I felt he was in an aggressive mood and I wanted to head him off by saying my piece.'

'Why, Luther?'

'I felt at that moment I was doing the right thing.'

'And what do you feel now?'

'It's probably a terrible thing to say, Tad, but I still think it was the right thing.'

'The end justifies the means? Hitler's old motto.'

Meynell didn't respond although philosophical and historical refutations crowded into his mind. At least Anders was under control so far.

Anders said quietly, 'And when are you going to tell Burinski?'

'Whoever it is, it won't be me, Tad. It has to be somebody official.'

Anders smiled grimly. 'That lets me out, then.'

'I suppose it does.'

Meynell was playing it by ear and he didn't like it. He'd come expecting anger and accusations and all he had hoped for was to damp them down. His scenario had not gone beyond that.

'What will they do with Burinski?'

'He'll go up to the place in Scotland.'

'I suggest that you prepare for a serious psychological shock when he's told.'

'The question of telling him hasn't been discussed with me. Has he finished talking as far as you're concerned?'

'We've covered everything except their communications system.'

'Would you be willing to carry on until you've got that?'

'I'd consider it if I was specifically asked to.'

Meynell looked across at him. 'Would you be prepared to break the news to Burinski instead of it being done formally?'

'And tell him we lied to him?'

'Would you really need to, Tad? Would it do any good? Wouldn't it be better to point out that if we made any attempt even to contact her she'd probably go straight to the Gulag because they'd know he'd talked?'

Anders shrugged. 'Who knows?'

'But you would cooperate?'

'Probably.'

'How about I take you to lunch?'

'I'm taking my girlfriend to lunch, but thanks.'

'How is she? Judy or Julie isn't it? I'm bad with girls' names.'

Anders smiled. 'Her name's Candy.'

'Sounds American.'

'Bethnal Green, actually.'

Anders walked with Meynell to the street door and after Meynell had merged into the crowds Anders walked back to his rooms and poured himself another whisky. He sat in his armchair with his feet up on the coffee table. He sat there composing a dozen variations of a resignation letter as he boiled with anger. Not about Burinski. He had known exactly how he would deal with that from the moment Meynell told him of the lie. His anger was at the indifference and callousness of people like Sir Arthur and Meynell. Especially Sir Arthur. That dried-up old maid, with his cold, venomous little mind. A mind that could throw him away with the same lack of compunction as he threw away Burinski. Not only him and Burinski, but anybody who wasn't needed or didn't fit in. For once he'd teach the bastards a lesson. And he'd do it their way.

French sat listening intently as Meynell reported on his meeting with Anders, and when he had finished he sat silent for several minutes, fiddling with a gilt letter-opener on his desk. When he looked up he said, 'Sounds as though you did surprisingly well, Luther. I'd expected one of those theatrical explosions of Slav temperament. My word is my bond and all that.'

'Not at all. He was calm and sensible, and as cooperative as any man could be in the circumstances.'

'I wonder why?'

'Oh, Arthur, let's not look our gift horse in the mouth. He surely deserves a pat on the back, not suspicion of his motives. He must despise us even if he understands. He could have left us high and dry *and* felt justified in doing so.'

'I expect you're right.' French paused. 'Will you talk to him? Ask him to continue until he's got all we want and then tell Burinski. He's getting off very lightly, is Burinski. Anders wouldn't have ended up in a Russian manor house with hotel food and women and the rest of it.'

'Yes. I'll talk to him.'

'You do whatever you think fit, but let me know if there are any real problems. I'd like to get it all over and done with.'

Meynell phoned Anders and found him still calm if slightly distant. Anders estimated that the rest of the debriefing would take a couple of weeks, maybe three, and had even thought that he might eventually get Burinski to go over the assassination on the spot. Checking the route and the houses where he had stayed. Meynell was relieved that Anders was taking it all in his stride.

Judy phoned and suggested they met in the bar at the Café Royal.

He got there early and ordered a whisky for himself and a Campari and soda for her. She kept him waiting for ten minutes and then swept in through the door, smiling as she hurried towards him. And suddenly he realised why he had always been held by her. She reminded him of Marie-Claire. Not her face, but her style. The clothes she wore, the way she walked and sat, and the movements of her arms. She was wearing a white dress that he guessed was Courrèges, her hair had been styled and set, and her feet in the black, pointed, court shoes looked small and neat. Several heads turned to look as she hurried towards him and then she was putting her mouth up to be kissed in a cloud of Chanel 19. As she sat down she draped a silver fox stole over the next chair, turning quickly to look at his face.

'You look very fit, Charles. Is this mine?' And she sipped the drink and made a smiling moue of disapproval.

'They're slipping Charles, too much soda. Tell me what you've been doing.'

He smiled. 'Nothing much. I was away for some time.'

'What was it? Business?'

'Yes. How about you?'

She looked at him, smiling. 'What on earth did you say to Mama when you two met?'

'Nothing special. Why?'

She laughed. 'You certainly made a hit there. She thinks you're fantastic. Not in front of Daddy, of course. But she didn't entirely desert you. Said you were very presentable. She said dishy to me. Said you looked reliable, and nothing like she had imagined.'

Anders smiled. 'What did he say?'

'Oh, dismissed it of course. Silly, impressionable woman. He should have dealt with you himself and all that sort of guff. What did you think of her?'

He laughed. 'It wasn't quite the sort of meeting where people are at their best. She was obviously scared of the whole thing. She said her piece. I was very uncooperative but when she felt that she had completed her task she was charming.'

‘She said it was a pity I hadn’t married you in the first place and then there would have been no problems.’

‘So now what?’

‘Can I have another Campari? So now what? I’m just going to sit it out, Charles. Mama’s on my side and she’ll keep working on him. She does have some influence. She’ll try and find some way of making it all seem more tolerable.’ She smiled and reached out to straighten his tie. ‘Why the parachutes?’

‘It’s a club tie. Special Forces Club.’

‘D’you like my dress?’

‘It’s beautiful. Is it Courrèges?’

‘Of course. Mama bought it for me. I put it on specially for you. It’s only the second time I’ve worn it.’

‘It suits you. You look very pretty.’

‘Thank you, kind sir.’ She turned to look around. ‘They’re taking their time with that drink.’ She turned back to him. ‘Are you going to feed me?’

‘I’ve booked us a table in the Grill.’

‘Lovely. By the way, we met some man who knows you. I can’t remember his name.’

‘Where was it?’

‘At the Inn on the Park. Some learned society or other. Frightful bore but good food. Daddy pumped him about you but the old boy wasn’t the pumpable kind. A bit old in the tooth but majestic; piercing eyes that kind of looked into you. I think his name was Mendl or maybe Menzies the Scottish way. Although I would have said there was Jewish blood somewhere there. Professor Mendl. Does that ring a bell?’

‘Was it Meynell? Professor Luther Meynell.’

‘That was it.’

And Anders smiled to himself at the thought of Luther Meynell’s reaction to being described as ‘an old boy’ and ‘long in the tooth’.

They ate and enjoyed a long pleasant meal and she retailed the gossip of embassy circles. Who was sleeping with whom, who had been caught out, who was making big money on the side because he could get licences that weren't obtainable, and even the amusing story of a man who loved his wife.

Her parents were still in town, still staying at the French Embassy and she was staying with them. She asked for a brandy, and as she sipped it Anders said, 'When can I see you again?'

Her big brown eyes looked back at him. 'I can't for the next two weeks but I'll phone you as soon as they've gone. I love you, Charles, and I think my Mama loves you too. But I'd better go, honey.'

He walked with her into Regent Street and the doorman waved down a taxi. As Anders opened the taxi door she slid her arms round his neck and put up her mouth to be kissed.

It was almost four in the morning as Anders put the canvas holdall and the case into the boot of the white MGC and turned the key in the lock. He had checked all the things a dozen times. He lifted the bonnet and unclipped the distributor head and slid it into his jacket pocket.

The alarm woke him at eight o'clock and he dressed slowly before he went into the small kitchen and pressed two fresh oranges for a drink. He drove up to the safe-house at Ebury Street just after ten, and told Burinski that he was taking him to Hammersmith to go over the details of the assassination. Burinski looked worried.

'Why do we need to do this when I've gone over all the details with you so many times?'

'When you see the various places it might remind you of something, Vasili. Something you'd forgotten.'

'I'm sure it won't.'

'We'll see. Anyway a trip outside might do you good.'

They were almost at Bromley before Burinski turned in his seat. 'Why does it take so long? I don't recognise anywhere. Where are we?'

Anders smiled. 'We're just having a little ride, Vasili. You must be tired of being cooped up in that place for so long.'

Burinski looked at him only half-believing, but he settled back in his seat.

As they turned off the Hastings road at the sign for Battle Anders glanced at Burinski and saw that he was asleep. He woke as Anders drove through the open gates that led up to the cottage garage.

As Anders took the case out of the boot he handed it to Burinski.

'That's yours, my friend.'

He reached for the holdall, pulled down the boot cover, took Burinski's arm and led him to the front door of the cottage.

For a fleeting moment he felt sad as they walked into the sitting room and he remembered his days there with Candy, but he brought his mind back to what he was doing and walked over to the drinks cabinet. He poured them both a large, neat whisky, handed one to Burinski and pointed to one of the chairs and sat in the facing one. He smiled and lifted his glass.

'*Na zdrovye.*'

Burinski smiled. '*Na zdrovye.*'

'I want to talk to you, Burinski. A serious talk. OK?'

Burinski nodded. 'OK.'

'If I hadn't been exchanged what would have happened to me?'

'I guess you'd have ended up in the Gulag.'

'How long for?'

Burinski shrugged. 'Who knows, comrade? Twenty years, thirty years. Maybe for life.

'Or maybe I would get one of those special injections and then they would bury me in that secret place near Smolensk. Yes?'

'Sometimes that happens.'

'If Moscow had been very generous and allowed me to choose between the injection and the Gulag which do you think I would have chosen?'

Burinski shrugged. 'How should I know that?'

'I said which do you *think* I should have chosen?'

'The Gulag.'

'Why?'

'Because you would think that maybe you could escape.'

'Would you have helped me escape?'

'My God. It would be impossible. How could I do that? Nobody has ever escaped. If they get out of a camp they die of exposure and starvation.'

'If I had talked to Kalin or you, what would have happened to me then?'

Burinski shifted uneasily in his seat and sipped his whisky before he looked back at Anders.

'The same. It would have made no difference.'

'They wouldn't have brought my girlfriend from London and let us live in Moscow?'

'No. That could never happen.'

Anders looked at Burinski's face and said softly, 'So why did you think that we should get your wife and child out and bring them to London?'

All the colour drained from Burinski's face and his hand trembled as he reached out to put his glass on the table.

'You mean you lied to me. And the man Nicholson lied?'

'No. We both told you the truth. Or what we thought was the truth. Other people lied to us.'

He saw the open fear in Burinski's eyes.

'You're going to kill me, comrade, that's why you've brought me here.'

'No. I'm not.'

'What then?'

'I'm going to help you escape.'

Burinski shook his head. 'I don't believe that.'

Anders produced the canvas holdall. 'There are two passports for you in there. There are other documents too, and there's money. Dollars and pounds.' He pointed at the case. 'There are new clothes for you in there.'

Burinski made no move to check what was in the holdall or the case but sat looking at Anders.

'What happens?'

'I'm going to get you out of the country. I'll go with you

part of the way, and tonight I'll tell you what you should do when you get to Berlin.'

'Why do they let me go?'

Anders smiled. 'They aren't letting you go, Vasili. *I'm* letting you go.'

'Without permission? Against your orders?'

Anders nodded. 'Yes.'

'And what happens to you?'

'I'll have to wait and see. I don't think anything will happen to me.'

'What news is there of Inge and the baby.'

'They're OK. We'll talk about all that this evening. I want you to change into your new clothes right away so that you'll get used to them.'

Candy's mother sat in the small room in the upright armchair that she had bought for seven shillings just before the war started. Despite the sunshine outside, the room had an air of twilight. A green chenille runner with scallops and bobbles was fastened to the high mantelpiece with big-headed brass tacks. A mahogany clock was in the centre and to the left was a good sized, decorated, japanned tin with 'Biscuits' on the front. Its similar companion on the right was marked 'Tea'. A low, metal candlestick with half a candle was at the far end, and there were several small photographs in cheap frames at the back of the mantelpiece.

Below was an old-fashioned coal range with an open fire and an oven. There was a trivet for a kettle on the top bar of the fire and on a firebrick lying on its side, the kettle itself in burnished copper.

The wallpaper was faded, but huntsmen, and ladies riding side-saddle were just discernible, and along one angle where the wall met the ceiling were the brown stains of damp above the picture rail.

Candy's mother was knitting, the glossy knitting pattern on her lap, and despite the misshapen joints of her arthritic fingers she knitted easily but slowly. To Victoria Amelia Price and many like her, knitting was more than a way of making sweaters and scarves. It was a therapy that took your mind off poverty and unemployment; and it worked. A cup of tea and a knitting pattern were her generation's equivalents of smoking pot or sniffing glue. Not quite oblivion but a half-way house.

As Candy lifted the teapot her mother said, 'Use the cloth or you'll burn yourself.'

'Do you want some biscuits or a sarnie?'

'No. Just pour the tea and sit down. Put the cosy on the teapot and it won't get cold.'

'Still no sugar?'

'No, not for me.'

Candy put the cup and saucer and a plate of fancy cakes near her mother and sat down.

'Mum.'

'Yes.'

'I've got something to tell you.'

'I know. Get on with it.'

'How did you know?'

Her mother laughed, and without looking up from her knitting she said, 'I know you, my girl. I can read you like a book. Always could. And that's no bad thing either.'

'Tad's asked me to marry him.'

Her mother went on knitting and Candy Price said, 'Why don't you say something?'

'You were telling me something, not asking me a question. If you want to ask me something, ask me.'

'Are you pleased?'

'He hasn't asked me child, he's asked you, and I gather you're pleased enough.'

'Oh I am, Mum. I love him so much.'

The old lady lifted her head and turned it to look at her daughter.

'And what does that mean?'

'What does what mean?'

'You say you love him. What's it mean?'

'You know what it means, and you know what I mean. You're just being awkward.'

'What do you want me to say? That he's attractive, strikes me as reliable and honest and will make you a wonderful husband?'

'No. I want to know if you think I'll make him a wonderful wife.'

'That's the first sensible thing you've said, little girl.'

'So tell me.'

Her mother put her knitting on the floor beside her and leaned back in her chair. She took off her glasses, wiped them on her pinafore and put them back on before she spoke. She smiled at her daughter.

'I'm glad he asked you. He's a nice man. He must think a lot of you to ask you. What did you say to him?'

'I told him I'd think about it before I said either "yes" or "maybe we'll wait for a bit".'

'You've got more sense than I gave you credit for. What about that other girl you told me about?'

'That's Judy. I don't think she would marry him. She's got a rich husband. She wants to leave him but I don't think she's got the guts to go through a divorce. She doesn't love Tad, anyway.'

'How do you know?'

'You can tell. When she's been with him at the club she never looks at him, she just wants to make sure who's looking at her. She puts him down, acts superior. She won't call him Tad. She thinks it's vulgar. She calls him Charles. That's his second name. And whatever he is Tad ain't a Charles. To my mind she's a real bitch and she'd make him unhappy.'

'Maybe that's what he wants. Those society girls know what the world's all about.'

'Do they hell. They're just the same as the rest of us. They just act like they're different.'

'Some of them *are* different.'

'How for God's sake?'

'They're better educated. Been to good schools and universities.'

'So what?'

Mrs Price reached out and put her hand on her daughter's

arm. 'What about his friends, love? They've all been to those Eton and Harrows and universities. How would you get on with them?'

'I'd do my best. They'd have to do their best with me.'

'But you wouldn't like it if they came the old acid with you, would you? You wouldn't keep your temper. There'd be scenes and embarrassment for Tad.'

'He'd stick up for me.'

'I'm sure he would, girl, and in the end he wouldn't see them any more. And he'd end up with no friends.'

'We could make our own friends.'

Her mother didn't answer but when she saw Candy's stricken face she said quietly, 'Why don't you compromise?'

'How?'

'Say yes but you want to wait for a bit. Live with him. See how it develops. Go out of your way to fit in. You and he'll get on fine, I'm sure of that, but you've both got to live in the daily world. If you really love him, see if you can't go a bit towards his sort of people.'

'I love you, Mum. You're always so kind to me. I don't know why you put up with me.'

'I don't, either. Why don't you bring him down for tea one of these days? I'll make a chocolate cake. Men always like those.'

Candy jumped up and rushed round to kiss her mother, and a few minutes later her mother heard her singing as she washed up the crockery in the tiny scullery. She was singing something about "My guy" and her mother shook her head slowly. So much beauty, so much lovingness, all going to waste. If she married Tad Anders it would be cherished and protected. But could she make the effort to fit in? To smile at those chic women and their smooth men? She couldn't have done it herself. All she'd had to get used to was supporting Spurs instead of Fulham, her father's team. The girl would have enough sense to know that there would be no more casual sleeping around. She understood the basics of men and women all right. It was just the glossy bit that might get her down. She sighed as she thought of what her husband would have said if he could hear her persuading her daughter to be nice to the toffs. He'd turn in his grave. His Candy was good enough for the Prince of Wales. He'd said so often enough. If she was going to stay the night she'd better air the bed with a hot-water bottle.

Some people are moved to tears by sunsets or Rachmaninov, and Mrs Price was moved to tears by a hot-water bottle. The new, big, blue one from Boots she put at the foot of the tiny single bed. The one shaped like a rabbit she put near the pillow, and she remembered so many nights when Harry had called her to see the blonde hair on the pillow and a small plump hand just outside the blanket, curved round that same rubber rabbit.

Burinski looked quite smart in his Marks and Spencers two-piece suit. A pale biscuit colour, with a slight flare to the trousers and unmistakeably English. Suede shoes and a cream shirt with a brown tie, and he could have been middle management for any company except IBM. He was obviously pleased with his new image.

There were various documents laid out on the coffee table between them. Anders was pointing at the two passports.

'One's British. The other's West German. Federal Republic. Except for the names they're both genuine. Nobody's going to stop you on suspicion they're forgeries. There's two hundred pounds in Sterling notes. A hundred US dollars and three hundred Deutsche Marks. OK?'

Burinski nodded. 'Yes. OK.'

'I'll be going with you as far as Ostend. We travel separately because they'll be looking for two men together when they do start looking. From Ostend you take a train to Brussels. You speak German when we get to Ostend and once we've landed you use your German passport.

'From Brussels you take a plane to Tegel. You fly only Sabena, Lufthansa or British Airways. No others. From Tegel you take a taxi into the city centre and then you take another taxi to Pension Frohnau. It's not a safe-house nor does it have any Intelligence connections, it's a place that lets out rooms by the hour or the night to prostitutes. Nobody will look at you too carefully.

'There's a guide service in the Kurfürstendamm called Severin and Kühn. They run guided bus tours into East Berlin. For that you use your British passport. After that I can't help you, but I guess you've got your own black-market contacts over the other side.'

Anders picked up an envelope. 'If you get them out or if you decide to settle down on your own in West Berlin, you take this envelope to the address on it and ask for the man named on the envelope. You don't give it to anybody except him. You ask him to read it while you wait. All he can do for you is get you documents so you can rent a room and get a job. You don't ever contact him again. He owes me a favour, but only one. If you play games you'll end up in the river. Understood?'

'Is there any way I can contact you?'

'No. When I've got you back I've done all I'm willing to do.'

Burinski looked at Anders across the table. 'Why are you doing this for me?'

Anders looked back at the Russian. 'You want the truth or a bunch of flowers?'

Burinski smiled. 'The truth of course.'

'I don't give a shit about you, Burinski. I'm doing this for your wife. She's got twice the guts you have. She's unlucky to have got involved with a bastard like you.'

Burinski smiled. A hard-eyed smile. 'You didn't ever bluff me, comrade. You think I don't already realise that this whole thing is set up by SIS. You made a good scenario but you make a mistake. One mistake.'

'Oh. What's that?'

Burinski pointed at the three small piles of money and then looked back at Anders.

'That's your mistake my friend. I make that three hundred and fifty pounds. Fourteen hundred D-marks. Nobody gives a stranger his own personal money to that amount. Why should you?'

Anders looked back at the Russian. 'Why the hell do you think SIS would spend public money on getting you out of the country?'

Burinski saw the barely controlled anger on Anders' face and in his voice. He shrugged.

'What does it matter?'

'You'd better get some sleep, Burinski. We shall be off early tomorrow morning.'

Burinski stood up, pointing at the things on the table. 'Do you want me to take those things?'

'They're all yours, comrade. Unless you'd like to go back to London.'

After Burinski had gone up to the spare bedroom Anders locked the door and went downstairs again. He moved one of the armchairs to the bottom of the stairs, took off his jacket and shoes, loosened his tie and made himself as comfortable as he could. All night he cat-napped in the chair.

Chapter 15

NICHOLSON GOT the call while he was still at the office and he tried to contact Sir Arthur but he was closeted with the Foreign Secretary, briefing him on Tel Aviv and Cairo prior to his Middle East trip. He tried the club but Anders had not been in the previous day or night. He had left no message nor told anyone that he would be away, but they were used to that. He was tempted to try Meynell but that would ruffle Sir Arthur's feathers. And there was nothing that they could say that would alter the facts. Burinski had gone out with Anders and hadn't come back. Anders wasn't at his club. It wasn't very difficult arithmetic.

The routine procedure was quite straightforward. All he had to do was notify Special Branch through MI5 liaison and pass them photographs of Anders and Burinski. And if he did that he might as well write out his resignation at the same time. Once the mincing machine started working it would no longer be in SIS's hands. Anders would be blown; unofficial and even unauthorised operations would be exposed. Not to the general public but to the critical and biased eyes of MI5. As in most countries in the world the Intelligence services were, from time to time, more suspicious of one another than their foreign rivals. But without the resources of Special Branch there was no equivalent in SIS to trace and find the two missing men. And Special Branch belonged to MI5 not SIS.

He phoned Stoppard at liaison and gave him a watered-down briefing on the situation and ordered him to organise his overseas people to drop what they were doing and spend time at ports and railheads looking out for Burinski. He made no mention of Anders and his orders were that if Burinski was identified they should make no contact with him but keep him under surveillance. Stoppard said quite openly that only luck could lead them to Burinski. They were too thin on the ground to do anything beyond going through the motions.

Nicholson phoned home to say that he would either be late or staying in town for the night and then turned back to his work. But his mind kept wandering to Anders. What the hell was he doing? And then Sir Arthur's secretary phoned to say that he was back and wanted to see him.

Sir Arthur was in a good mood, packing his case to take back to his cottage for the weekend.

'Peter. D'you have anything about a KGB man named Kuznetsov? Initials A.V.'

'Where is he?'

French smiled. 'At this moment he's sitting in Saunder's office in the Embassy in Ankara. He's already talking. You'd better contact Saunders and give him your priorities. I gather he can cover Israel, Iran, the Lebanon, Saudi Arabia and Egypt.'

'I'll do that, Sir Arthur. Can you spare me a few minutes?'

'Of course.' French went on putting things down in his case.

'Anders took Burinski out to check the details of the assassination yesterday morning. They left about ten and they haven't come back.'

Sir Arthur stopped fiddling with his clothes in the case but he didn't look at Nicholson.

'What have you done about it, Peter?'

'I've given Stoppard a very bowdlerised scenario, only mentioning Burinski, and told him to put all his men on ports and airports and railheads for a few days.'

'Did you mention Anders?'

'No.'

'Have you informed Five or Special Branch?'

'No, sir.'

'What do you think's going on?'

'I've no idea. It doesn't make sense.'

Sir Arthur turned to look at Nicholson who was amazed by his calmness.

'You're wasting Stoppard's men's time, Peter. Just contact

Pritchett in Berlin and tell him to put round-the-clock surveillance on Tegel and when he sees Burinski tell him to contact me personally and I'll deal with it myself.'

'You think that . . .'

'Let's not speculate, Peter. Put your thoughts on the little man in Ankara. He's more important than Burinski.'

'Maybe I should go out for a couple of days and brief Saunders?'

'It's entirely up to you. By the way, I saw your father the other night. He tells me he's thinking of early retirement. I was surprised.'

Nicholson laughed softly. 'He promises or threatens retirement once a year. He's just doing a Sinatra. A last and final appearance every June when he gets his second tax application. I'm sure he doesn't mean it.'

'I must say he sounds very convincing although I'd heard from reliable sources that he was being tapped for the Appeals Court.'

'Did you tell him that?'

'Good God, no. And you musn't either.'

'You'll be at the cottage all the weekend?'

'Yes. I'll take Michelmore as duty officer so the phone will be manned full time.'

'D'you need a lift to Liverpool Street?'

'That's kind of you. No. I'm dining first.'

'Have a good weekend.'

'And you. My regards to all your ladies.'

Nicholson walked slowly back to his own office. He had expected an explosion. Luther Meynell had often said that Sir Arthur was not only unpredictable but that that was one of his virtues. He behaved as if it didn't matter. But he must have at least thought vaguely of the possibility that Anders had lifted Burinski deliberately. And there was only one motive that he could think of for Anders to do that.

Anders washed and shaved and then walked out of the kitchen door. He stood, breathing in the cool, early-morning air. Across the valley the sky was grey, but it was the grey that promised a hot sunny day and a calm flat Channel. He went back into the kitchen and poured the last of the coffee into the china mugs and took one up to Burinski.

At Dover he garaged the car near the ferry terminal and they walked to the embarkation area with half an hour to spare.

Anders kept Burinski in sight for most of the journey and was only a few feet in front of him as he went through customs and immigration at Ostend. But on the cobbled quay-side Burinski was trembling.

'What's the matter, my friend?'

'He asked me the purpose of my visit.'

'They always do that. You'll either say "Business" or "pleasure". He doesn't give a damn which you say.'

'I answered him in Russian. I was tensed up and I'd rehearsed what to say. I'd been thinking in Russian and it just came out.'

'What happened?'

'He went through my passport again. Page by page. And then he took it to another man and they checked in a book. The other man came back with him and asked me what my business was. I told him I was only in transit. That I was going to Düsseldorf via Brussels because I'd never seen Brussels before. He kept looking at me. And he hesitated before he gave me back my passport.'

'Which one did you use?'

'Like you said. The British one.'

'So what's the problem?'

'I'll never make it to Berlin. I nearly ran away.'

'D'you like strawberry tarts, Burinski?'

Burinski looked shocked. 'I don't understand.'

'A simple question. Do you like strawberry tarts?'

'I've never had one.'

'There's a café in the Rue Longue that sells the best strawberry tarts in Europe. We're going to have one each right now.'

Burinski found that he didn't like strawberry tarts and

as Anders finished up Burinski's tart he said, 'How are you going to get on in Berlin, comrade?'

'I'll be more at home there. I know my way around.'

'Have you got contacts in West Berlin?'

Burinski nodded. 'One or two.'

'What about East Berlin?'

'Yes, but I shan't use those unless I'm desperate.'

'How are you going to contact Inge?'

'I shall try and contact her parents down south and see what I can find out from them.'

'They'll be watching them too.'

'And there's my father in Moscow.'

Anders shook his head. 'You're playing games with a lot of people's lives, Burinski.'

Burinski shrugged. 'Will you come with me to Berlin? Just to Tegel. That's what scares me most of all. If the West Germans got me . . .' he shrugged and fell silent.

'I'll go with you to Berlin, but after that you're on your own. What you do is up to you. If you take my advice you'll get somewhere to live in West Berlin, and a job and you'll sit the time out. If you really care about your wife you won't go near her. Wait a year or two years until it's almost forgotten.' Anders stood up. 'Let's get to the station.'

They were in Brussels by noon and took a train out to the airport. There was a Lufthansa flight to Düsseldorf in an hour and a connection to Berlin in the late evening.

The DC10 landed at Berlin-Tegel exactly at midnight and was the last scheduled flight of the day. Burinski kept close to him as they walked across the tarmac. Burinski survived the cursory inspection by the immigration officers and they were at the baggage inspection when Anders glanced towards the reception area. There were only half a dozen people there and he didn't recognise any of them. It was only when he turned his back to the customs desk that he saw him. It was Andy Pritchett, standing at the bar with a glass in his hand. For a moment he thought Pritchett had seen him but he had turned to order another drink, chatting up the bar-girl. Anders turned back to the customs officer and said that his other case had not come off the aircraft. He was referred to one of the Lufthansa ground staff.

He took Burinski with him and they sat in the Lufthansa freight office for nearly two hours while the aircraft hold was checked. He was apologetic about his baggage tag being missing but the search had gone on with Lufthansa thoroughness until Anders suggested that he would call back later that day to see if his case had been traced. Lufthansa were going to contact Düsseldorf and Brussels in case it had been misrouted.

Back in the flight reception area Anders could see that the bar and restaurant were in darkness and as they walked out of the big glass doors Anders headed Burinski away from the exit route past the closed airline desks and the shops to the incoming unloading doors.

Outside there were several waiting taxis but the concourse was empty. He looked across at the car park. There were a dozen cars, all empty, and he went straight to the second taxi, and as he pushed Burinski inside he asked for Hotel Windsor in Knesebeckstrasse.

Twenty minutes later Anders paid off the driver and stood talking to Burinski until the taxi had left and then they walked to the other end of the street and Anders rang the night bell of the Plaza.

There were no single rooms so they settled for a double with twin beds. Burinski asked why Anders had gone through the charade about the missing case and Anders merely told him that it was to avoid going through with the other passengers on the flight. Andy Pritchett, was too busy with the bar-girl, thank God. She was pretty enough for Pritchett, and he'd probably gone over to chat with her until she was off duty.

Anders was up early the next morning and when he was dressed he left Burinski still asleep and walked to the corner and turned right into the Kurfürstendamm.

Although it was only just 7.30 the broad pavement was already busy with people hurrying to work. Shop windows were being washed down and dustmen were clearing containers of rubbish followed by a street-cleaning team. At Uhlandstrasse he turned right and then another right turn at the end of the block into Lietsenburger Strasse. At the corner of Knesebeckstrasse Anders stopped.

Cars were queuing for the multi-storey carpark, a small post office van was parked just beyond and workmen were digging deep into the road fifty yards further on. There was a smell of stale gas from the red clay soil. There were several people waiting for their employers to open up their shops, and an elderly woman was unloading bunches of flowers from a green van into baskets and pans in the shadow of two plane trees.

Anders walked slowly to stand under the spreading branches of the trees. His eyes were on a dark blue BMW parked on the other side of the street about thirty metres before the hotel. A man sat in the driver's seat, the window was down and his arm rested on the car door. He had a pipe in his mouth but it wasn't lit, and round his thick wrist was a leather band. The kind of wrist-support sometimes worn by men who had to shove their fellow men around. Anders watched for ten minutes as the man sat there unmoving. And he sat with the patience and stillness of a man who was used to sitting and waiting.

Anders walked slowly up to the Ku'damm and stood on the corner. He bought a newspaper and as he turned to walk back down the street the car started up and came towards him. As it passed he saw the man's face. It was round and flabby but deeply tanned with a frieze of black hair that flowed down to heavy side-burns. Anders had never seen him before and the man didn't even glance at him as he passed.

Anders looked at his watch. The shops would be open and he walked on down the Ku'damm to the travel agency. There was a flight to Brussels leaving at eleven and an onward connection to Ostend half an hour after arrival. They couldn't book him cross-channel but suggested that he check with the Lufthansa desk at Brussels. He paid for his ticket and slid it into his jacket pocket, feeling in reflex for the holster that wasn't there.

Burinski was dressed and waiting, anxious to talk, but Anders had had enough of him and hurried him down to the desk and paid their bill.

There was a taxi off-loading new arrivals at the hotel entrance and Anders gave the address of Pension Frohnau. Burinski seemed to be under control, and with an enthusiasm bordering on euphoria he assured Anders that he had it all worked out in his head. When the taxi stopped Anders pointed out the Pension Frohnau and Burinski picked up his case and got out of the taxi. At the open door he was grinning as he held out his hand. Reluctantly Anders took it, but he neither wished Burinski good luck nor bade him goodbye. He turned to the driver as he closed the car door and told him to take him to Tegel.

At the bookstall he bought copies of *Stern* and *Time* magazines. He sat in the white-tiled toilets until his plane was called.

They were late arriving at Brussels and there was no time to check on the ferries, but at Ostend there was no problem. The ferry was half empty.

At Dover he paid for the garaging of his car and an hour and a half later he pulled up at the cottage. For almost fifteen minutes he sat there, then he started the car again and headed for the A21 and London.

It was 3 a.m. when he turned into the mews at the back of the club. There was the usual array of garbage and overflowing dustbins and a Ford Cortina with a couple in the back seat. Anders wondered what kind of people chose such tatty surroundings for their courting. The man's face was in shadow but the girl looked quite pretty.

He walked round to the entrance to the club. The door was locked and padlocked and as he unlocked he realised how tired he was. The pain in his chest was there again, not severe, but persistent. He locked the doors behind him and switched on the lights as he walked down the stairs and through to his own rooms. He left the lights burning, too tired to close off the control switches.

He was in the bath when the phone rang, his eyes closed

and almost asleep. He got out and put his bathrobe over his shoulders as he walked into the sitting room.

'I heard you were back, Tad.'

It was Nicholson, and Anders half-smiled.

'Who was it, Peter? The couple in the Cortina?'

'I'd better come over and see you later today. How about this afternoon at three?'

'That's OK, Peter.'

'Are you all right, Tad?'

'I'm fine.'

'Are you on your own?'

'Yes.'

'You'd better get some sleep in before the balloon goes up.'

'You too, comrade.'

Anders heard Nicholson's quiet laugh and hung up.

Nicholson looked at the wine in his glass as he spoke.

'What do you think Sir Arthur's going to do about it, Tad?'

Anders shrugged. 'I'm not much worried, Peter. I've written out my resignation.'

'You can't resign, Tad, you aren't on the establishment.'

'I've recognised that. I've just said that I've finished working for them.'

'Tell me why? Did you really care all that much about what happened to Burinski?'

'I didn't give a damn about what happened to Burinski.'

'So what was it?'

'French sent me into Berlin with no back-up to get Burinski out. When *he* wanted Burinski out it was a full-scale operation. I've had enough of that kind of thinking.'

'For God's sake, Tad. Sir Arthur authorised the exchange for you. Surely that squares the account?'

'Does it?'

'Why not?'

Anders stood up and slid off his jacket and when he sat down again he slowly unbuttoned his shirt and pulled it open. Nicholson saw the deep well-muscled chest and the white patch on the tanned skin where the rib had pierced the flesh and the long concave recess where half the rib was missing.

He looked back to Anders' face. 'I still don't understand, Tad. It's ghastly, but I don't see the connection with Burinski.'

'It's nothing to do with Burinski. He's just a symbol.'

'Of what?'

'It's a message from me to Sir Arthur. And to you for that matter. A protest, if you like. You two, and others, sit there in your offices and decide what happens to me and other field agents. And when you work it out it's a balance sheet. Debits and credits. But there's something missing in the arithmetic. Nobody takes account of what the man in the trap might want. You salve your consciences by warning us right at the start that you won't lift a finger to help us once we're in the bag. The KGB do more for their agents than you do for us. Just for once your little sums have been spoiled. I spoiled them. Deliberately. And you and French can do what the hell you like about it.'

Nicholson sat in silence for several minutes. Then he looked across at Anders before he spoke.

'Before I say what I really want to say let me make it clear that I've got great respect for you. Not only as an operator but as a man. I haven't got your physical courage and I'm not sure that I've even got your moral courage. It may seem strange to you but I'm proud of working with you. I may not always show it and for most of the time I'm not even conscious of it. But it's there. I don't have any doubt that Sir Arthur feels much the same. He's older than you and me, so he's less tolerant of some things, but when the chips are down you're one of his men and he'll be on your side, fighting. Not with his fists because it isn't necessary. But with a very bright mind that knows its way around the Whitehall rule-book and cheats when it's necessary.

'However . . .' Nicholson paused and smiled. 'How I hate people who say "however". However, I've never heard such rubbish as in your little homily. It was just hearts and flowers, gypsy violins and bleeding hearts. You make up your mind in absolute ignorance of the facts. You know your side of the story and you're not only ignorant about the other side, but you don't even realise that there *is* another side.'

Nicholson leaned forward and poured himself more wine and when he looked up Anders saw his anger showing in the muscles round his mouth and jaw as he started to speak again.

'Let me give you a few facts, Tad. Do you know what TACFIRE is?'

Anders shook his head.

'TACFIRE is an eyes-only US army system that automates firing instructions for field artillery units. A contract has just been placed with a US company to design digital plotters for TACFIRE. It's worth about 2.4 million dollars. Understand?'

'Yes.'

'Good. We heard rumours that the Soviets had already designed such a system. We weren't sure if the rumours were true but we spent a lot of time and money working on a KGB man who would know. We discovered that they had such a system and we spread a net for the KGB man and we picked him up in Amsterdam. At first he refused to talk, but slowly we were breaking through. We reckoned that in a few weeks he would cooperate. Sir Arthur had this operation very much under his control. If it worked it was going to save maybe two years research and several million dollars. And we should share the technology with the Americans. The name of the Russian was Gorlinski. He was the man Moscow wanted in exchange for you. The decision was entirely Sir Arthur's. He didn't consult anybody or get anybody's permission or suggest to anyone that maybe the exchange should be refused. I told him who they wanted in exchange for you. He just nodded and told me to agree. So much for your martyrdom.

'Next point. Your present little escapade. When I had to report to French that you and Burinski were missing, he didn't panic or call in Special Branch which would have meant real trouble for you. I couldn't understand why he took it so calmly, but he did. And when I phoned him to say that you were back and minus Burinski he told me to come along and see you. To reassure you that no action was being taken against you. He told me to ask you to stand by for an assignment that's likely to come up in about four weeks. That's your ogre, Tad.'

Anders shrugged. 'That's just *your* gypsy music, Peter.'

Nicholson laughed. 'OK. OK. Maybe I didn't phrase it very well. There's gypsy music on both sides and maybe my side hasn't played you enough music week by week. We do understand, Tad. But there's not all that much we can do. We can't keep saying we love you every day.'

'Just a greetings card a couple of times a year would do.'

Nicholson knew then that Anders had absorbed what he had said. Not convinced, but the feathers had been smoothed down enough for them to gradually get things back to normal. On the whole the life suited Anders and he must know it. And what else would he do?

'Will you come and stay with us for the weekend?'

'I'll be with my girlfriend.'

'Which one?'

'Candy.'

'The smashing blonde from downstairs?'

'That's the one.'

'Why not bring her with you?'

'Are you sure?'

'Of course I'm sure, we'd love to have you both.'

'OK.'

Nicholson smiled. 'Are the back-room boys forgiven?'

'No. But I've taken the point.'

'Fair enough. Are you coming by car to our place?'

'Yes.'

'OK. Friday, any time after lunch.'

They were sitting at the table nearest to the piano. It wasn't a popular table. Members only took it if all the other tables were full. They complained that they had to raise their voices while the piano was playing, and what they were generally talking about wasn't meant to be said that loud. Baldy was singing quite softly, extolling the virtues of Mott Street in

July, and Tad Anders was watching the girl's face as she looked up from her drink.

'Did you enjoy the weekend?'

'It was smashing, Tad. They're wonderful people. Not snobby at all.'

Anders smiled. 'Did you think they would be?'

She shrugged. 'I wasn't sure. I thought in little ways they might be. All that jazz about which knife to use and the stuff about wines and vintages. I didn't want to let you down.'

'Who did you like best?'

'I couldn't say. I liked them all for different reasons. I think maybe Peter's mother. She's a toucher. She patted my knee and touched my arm and talked as if she was really interested in me. I liked Peter because he's very dishy but I don't think he knows it. Doesn't cash in on it anyway. And the old judge was marvellous. Sat there with his head on one side, all solemn as I tried to explain the difference between jazz and reggae. Me the expert, him the student. And they're so polite. Even to one another. I loved it.'

'The judge took me on one side and said I ought to have a portrait painted of you in a white dress in a garden. Perhaps sitting on a swing, he said.' He smiled. 'You didn't mention Fleur.'

'I know. She's very beautiful and elegant and chic and she's obviously crazy about Peter but somehow . . . I don't know . . . not my cup of tea.'

'Why not?'

'Reminds me a bit of Judy. A bit self-important. A bit superior. Very much the gracious hostess, the lady of the house, and don't you forget it. Untouched by human hand. Not sure whether she's the fairy princess or the Ice Queen.'

'She said she thought you were an absolute doll.'

'That's exactly what I mean. If you said *she* was an absolute doll she'd take it as an insult. Dolls are in the Third Division at the bottom of the table, struggling against relegation to dumb blondes.'

Anders smiled. 'A bit catty, but not a bad assessment, sweetie.'

'It was catty. She was a very good hostess. She came into my bedroom that first evening. Quizzed me a bit about you. Asked if we were going to get married.'

'What did you say?'

She laughed. 'I told her I'd got my eye on Peter.' She smiled at her thoughts. 'For a moment she didn't know what to say and turned the conversation to clothes and perfume. I can hold my corner on those.'

He reached across the table for her hand and looked at her face. 'And are you going to marry me, Candy?'

'I talked about it with Mum, and I've thought about it so much, and I've tried to work out how to say it, but I can't.'

'Why can't you say it?'

'Oh, Tad. I've thought it all out so carefully and I know how it's going to be, but I wish it wasn't.'

'Just tell me, sweetie.'

She sighed. 'The answer's "yes", Tad. I'll marry you. I wish it could be tonight, but I want to suggest something. Let's live for a few months as if we are married and see how it goes. See if I fit in properly.'

'Let's do that, my love. But you don't have to fit in. I'm asking you just as you are right now. There ain't no exams to pass. I'd reckon I was very lucky to get you.'

'D'you mean that, Tad?'

'You bet I mean it.'

'It's a long time – the rest of our lives. And I want to make sure that I'll not spoil you life in any way.'

'In what way?'

'Your friends. People like the Nicholsons.'

'The Nicholsons. Why them?'

'They're well off. Well-educated. Upper class. They'd wonder what you saw in me.'

Anders laughed. 'They've seen you and they'll be quite sure they know why I grabbed you. Of course they'd only be partly right.'

'Tell me.'

'It's impossible to explain. It does matter to me that you're so pretty, but it's much more than that. When I'm with you it's like being in a nice warm bath. I feel much the same about Nicholson as you do. I guess I'm almost as well-off as he is. But because he comes from his sort of background it seems right that he's well-off, but for me it just feels like an accident. Good luck. He's not a snob. He treats me absolutely as an equal. But like you, I don't *feel* an equal. And we're not equal, we're different. He's not better than me, nor am I better than him. I could live much like he does, but I don't want to. It's not sour grapes. You liked his family and his home just as much as I did, but you wouldn't want it. And he doesn't expect me to be like him. You and I are much the same as one another. There's not going to be any problems with other people.'

'Don't tempt me, Tad, don't make me weaken, I need to do it. It's a kind of wedding present from me to you.'

'Speaking of presents, I've got one for you.'

'What is it?'

He fished in his pocket, and brought out a small envelope with the Royal crest on it and put it in front of her.

He smiled at her excitement as she loosened the seal and she looked up at him as she saw the square blue box. And she gasped as she pushed back the hinged lid and looked at the ring in its blue plush fitting. It was gold and there were five diamonds that flared even in the club's dim lighting.

She looked up at him. 'Oh, Tad. It's beautiful. Can I wear it?'

'Of course you can. Try it on.'

And then she turned it. 'There are some words engraved inside.' She smiled. 'I can make out Candy but I can't understand the other words.' She looked at his face. 'What does it say?'

'It says – *Kochana Candy, Ja ciebie kocham*. It's Polish.'

'What does it mean?'

'It means 'Darling Candy, I love you.'

She leaned across the table to kiss him and Joey appeared with an envelope in his hand. She spread out the fingers of her left hand and gave Anders the ring.

'You put it on, Tad.'

He slid it on to the third finger because although it wasn't even the correct hand for Polish custom it was what they did in England.

He turned and looked at Joey who offered him the envelope.

'A taxi-driver brought it, Mr Anders. It's addressed to you.'

There was a scribbled note and a press cutting. The note was hand-written.

> Tad,
>
> I thought you should see this. I hope it's not too much of a surprise but I guess you must have known from the start that it wasn't on. I've spoken to A. F. and there'll be no come-back. It looks as if all the accounts are square now.
>
> Fleur and the girls send you their love.
>
> Peter

He unfolded the newspaper cutting. It was from the *Berliner Zeitung*. There was a picture of Burinski's face. The eyes closed. The text covered four columns about four inches deep. The headline was thick and black.

> MYSTERY DEATH
>
> West Berlin police are appealing to the public for help in identifying the man in the photograph (inset). At approximately 6 p.m. yesterday evening this man collapsed in Fasanenstrasse about fifty metres from the junction with the Kurfürstendamm. Two onlookers, whose identity has not been disclosed, have made statements to the effect that they saw the man approached by two men who spoke to him briefly and then hurried to a black Volkswagen which was parked in the street nearby. The deceased collapsed and an ambulance was called but the unidentified man was dead on arrival at the hospital.
>
> First indications lead the police to consider that foul play cannot be ruled out. The victim appears to have died from asphyxiation but further medical examinations are due to take place.

The identity papers on the victim were found to be forgeries and it is considered possible that the man may have been involved in black-market or other criminal activities. Extensive checks are being carried out using the newly installed Central Police Records computer based in Wiesbaden.

Any member of the public who believes he has seen the man in the photograph should contact the nearest police station or the Kriminaldirektion (Tel. No. 78 1071).

Anders folded up the newspaper cutting and put it back in the envelope with Peter Nicholson's note. He'd been wrong. Andy Pritchett *had* seen him. He would have contacted London and they would have passed the word to Moscow. And now everybody was happy. Except . . .

Anders looked across at Candy Price. 'Have you got that nice white dress in your case upstairs? The one with the fringe?'

She laughed. 'Yes, I have.'

'Let's go upstairs. You put it on. I'll clean myself up and we'll go out for a meal.'

'Where shall we go?'

'We'll try the Connaught, sweetie. They do a very good steak and kidney pie. Not as good as your mother's, but good enough for us.'